SEX CRIMES

Jenefer Shute was born in South Africa. She received her
Ph.D. in Literature from UCLA and currently teaches at
Hunter College, where she is a professor of English. She is
also the author of *Life-Size*. She lives in New York City.

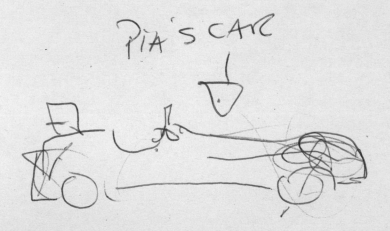

BY JENEFER SHUTE

Life-Size
Sex Crimes

Jenefer Shute

SEX CRIMES

VINTAGE

Published by Vintage 1998

2 4 6 8 10 9 7 5 3 1

First published in Great Britain by
Martin Secker & Warburg Limited 1997

Vintage
Random House, 20 Vauxhall Bridge Road,
London SW1V 2SA

Random House Australia (Pty) Limited
20 Alfred Street, Milsons Point, Sydney
New South Wales 2061, Australia

Random House New Zealand Limited
18 Poland Road, Glenfield,
Auckland 10, New Zealand

Random House South Africa (Pty) Limited
Endulini, 5A Jubilee Road, Parktown 2193, South Africa

Random House UK Limited Reg. No. 954009

A CIP catalogue record for this book
is available from the British Library

ISBN 0 09 926818 3

Papers used by Random House UK Ltd are natural, recyclable products made from wood grown in sustainable forests. The manufacturing processes conform to the environmental regulations of the country of origin

Printed and bound in Great Britain by
Cox & Wyman, Reading, Berkshire

SEX CRIMES

1

These are the parts I do recall:

I remember the red Sheraton sign on the skyline, how it throbbed through my window afterwards. I remember dialing 911 and waiting calmly on the window seat as the sirens wailed towards me. I remember the fire engine pulling up in the street below, the wheeze of its brakes, the mutter and crackle of its radio. I'd called for an ambulance, not a fire engine, obviously, but for some reason the city of Boston always sends all three at once—police, fire, ambulance. Don't know why. Perhaps people can't always tell what kind of help they need.

I remember the police car screeching past, making a U-turn, and stopping at an odd diagonal across Commonwealth Avenue, with both doors flung open like wings. I remember the ambulance rocking around the corner on two wheels. Three radios squawking now, firemen milling around looking for something to do, lights going on all over the block. I remember going downstairs to let the paramedics in.

That's all. Oh, yes, and I remember how cold I felt, teeth chattering, my bare arms splotched with crimson from the Sheraton sign.

That's all. Nothing else about that night. I know that's what the accused (or the very drunk) always say—I don't remember, Your Honor, I must have blacked out—but in my case it happens to be true. Oh, I'm not claiming to suffer from multiple personality or anything like that, though sometimes I wish I did, given the one I'm saddled with. I'm simply claiming that I *don't recall*—almost as if I hadn't been there at the time, as if I'd been out of the room or otherwise engaged. Which of course I was not: I've admitted that much already. I was the one who called the ambulance, after all, who stood with the police in the pulsing blue light.

No, what I mean is more complicated, more elusive than that. My lawyer has warned me against sounding like too much of an intellectual, but nevertheless I do feel compelled to mention a book I once read, a book about psychopaths. I've read quite a few books about psychopaths, actually, for reasons I hope to explain later. Anyway, this particular book quoted a murderer who confessed to his crime—but then added, by way of explanation: "Someone else did it, someone I've never known."

He wasn't denying his actions, you see, just attempting to characterize them. Perhaps you understand what I (and the psychopath) mean, perhaps not. My lawyer, for one, doesn't, but then I hardly expected her to; I know something about the way lawyers' minds work, being one myself.

Having been one myself, perhaps I should say.

My lawyer has also warned me against facetiousness; it sounds, she says, as if I'm not taking my situation seriously enough. My God, I say, I am, I *am* taking it seriously, how could I not? It's just that, under stress, I have an unfortunate tendency to crack jokes, the way another person might bite her nails or twitch. It's a tic, I tell her. OK, she says, with a shrug, but you're going to have to watch that. The tabloids are already doing their best to turn you into some kind of monster—*Fury* and so on. We have to keep reminding them, and everyone else, that they're dealing with a human being here.

Two human beings, I remind her.

Two human beings, she echoes, although, she adds, it doesn't necessarily help our case to emphasize that. What our case will be is still unclear: she thinks self-defense is the way to go—there's precedent, she claims—but her colleagues, feminists of a different stripe, think temporary insanity might be the better bet.

Whatever. My area of expertise is immigration law.

Was. Now I wish I'd mastered the criminal code.

I've been accused of so many offenses lately that I can hardly keep track—of professional misconduct, for instance, alcoholism, Prozac abuse. I've been accused of frigidity and erotomania, of arrested development and premature menopause, not to mention, of course, coloring my hair. I've been called a stalker, a spinster, a spitfire, and a Fury. The term *pathological liar* has been bandied about. I've been charged with assault, and, as you probably know, with worse. Much worse.

So be it. But allow me to ask you, in the spirit of disinterested clinical inquiry, as I now must ask myself: could one person really be culpable of so much? Could I?

My lawyer thinks it might help to write things down, construct a chronology. She's probably hoping that I'll start having flashbacks once I do, nice lurid ones that will help our defense. I doubt it. I ask her how I can construct a chronology if I don't remember what happened, let alone in what order. She hands me a yellow pad and a blue ballpoint and says, "Try."

I test the ballpoint and ask for a black marker instead, with an ultrafine tip. She finds me one.

"Your first meeting with the complainant," she says, handing it to me, uncapped.

THAT'S EASY: NEW Year's Eve, Angelica's loft, three or four A.M., on the downswing by then, feeling spaced out and cored, as if everyone around me— the beepered boy in the Gaultier suit, the aging girl in her bondage gear, the drag queen with one broken heel—had become a hallucination. Or, alternatively, that I had.

Finding my way to the bedroom mirror, I confirmed, by staring hard at my blotchy drained face, that I was indeed drunk. My skin, which was pale at the best of times, had a greenish cast: I tried to address the problem with Angelica's lipstick, but a slash of vermilion only made it worse. I tugged down my short black skirt, which was riding electrically up my thighs, and decided that, for me, the party was over. I'd have one more drink, kiss Angelica goodnight, and hop a cab home.

After a few minutes, I managed to catch Angelica's eye across the room and, inclining my head to
the door, pantomimed the idea of leaving; she gri-
maced and, making a don't-move-yet gesture, began
to squirm through the crowd, holding a cigarette in
one hand and a champagne flute high in the other.
Just then, someone yelled "Kristy!" and I saw she
meant me. "Chris?" I asked modestly, as if willing
to stand corrected on the question of my own name.
Who she might be, I hadn't a clue. Platinum hairdo,
Marilyn lips, great pointy-bra'd breasts. . . .
"Brenda!" I cried, remembering them. She'd been
black-dyed and ghoulish before, waiting tables at a
trendy little place where I sometimes stopped for a
drink, but now, she told me, she had a stand-up
routine. "It's about growing up Mormon," she said,
"you'll have to come see."

By the time I'd assured her that I would, I would,
and she'd assured me that, by the way, I looked
great, and she'd headed toward the kitchen to find a
lime for her Perrier—no more booze for her, those
days were long gone—and I'd moved on to the bar
again, Angelica was nowhere in sight. So I poured
myself one last Stoli, why not, and shouldered my
way, spilling some, through the crowd, scouting for

a familiar laugh or flash of bare flesh. I cruised the long table littered with baguette crumbs and olive pits, before remembering that Angelica never ate when she drank. I waited for a while by the bathroom door, but no-one came out, though I could hear at least three different kinds of giggle inside. Taking a final wincing sip from my drink, I poured the rest into a potted plant, from which, as a decorative touch, I then dangled the cup. When it slid off and hit the floor, I gave up on that project and sank into a small green love seat, striving to recall where I had left my coat.

"There you are," someone said, startling me, materializing from the right and dropping, splay-legged, onto the other end of the couch. "I've been looking for you."

"I've been here all along," I replied, trying to figure out who the hell he was. He looked vaguely familiar, but then so did most of Angelica's friends, who tended either to work at fashionable restaurants or to display themselves there. He was young, dark, very drunk, with short rough hair, blue-green-grey eyes—couldn't tell in that light—and a full, sullen mouth. His jeans were ripped across the knees, an affectation that annoyed me, especially in winter. He was compact and muscular, with a full-body slouch; a hands-in-pockets kind of guy, not my type at all.

"Scott," he said, realizing that I couldn't place him. "We met."

"Ah yes," I said, still blank. And then, reluctantly: "Chris."

"I know," he said, draining a plastic cup of what looked like Jack Daniel's, then holding the rim of the empty cup between his lips while he folded his arms across his chest. He flapped the cup up and down a few times, in lieu of conversation. It slipped out and fell on his lap.

"Nice," I said.

Still without a word, he leaned back, yawned and stretched, then began, ostentatiously, to knead the muscles behind his neck, rolling his head from side to side like an actor doing warm-up exercises.

"Stiff neck?" I asked, amused, recognizing my cue.

He nodded, still rolling, making a sharp little "Ahhh!" when he rolled too far.

"Rough night?"

"No," he said. "It's from hauling my equipment around, I think."

OK, I thought, I'll play.

"You in a band?" I asked.

"Nah," he said. "Used to be in one but now I'm trying to make it as a photographer. For *Things*, mostly." It figured: Angelica did most of the design work for *Things*, which had begun life as a radical weekly and ended up as a hip but postliterate guide to urban consumption.

"Hmmn," I said again, letting my gaze roam the room while in my mind I prepared my exit line.

"I read about you," he said. "In the *Globe*. I recognize you from the picture."

"God," I said, "I hope not." The most recent piece had been about the Haitian project, and the photographer had caught me at my most stern and self-righteous, wagging a pen.

"Your hair's a bit longer now," he said, then "Ouch." He was still trying to de-kink his neck, cocking it parrot-style to one side.

"You should try doing this," I suggested, bowing my head while pulling gently, overhand, on the base of my skull.

"It gets me right *there*," he said, then reached over and demonstrated with a heavy warm hand on the back of my neck. An army of tiny feet marched instantly down my spine, with small contingents peeling off along my arms and the backs of my thighs. My skin and nipples contracted, as if chilled.

I raised my head and looked him in the eye. He looked unblinkingly back at me. Some kind of nasty pang scrabbled around inside me. I looked away.

"I suppose you want me to offer you a back rub," I said, to recoup, "but really, that's such a lame approach."

He laughed, surprised. "No," he said, "not a *back* rub. That's not quite what I had in mind." He managed to look, at that moment, both cocky and callow, not without appeal.

"Whatever," I replied, shrugging, feeling in some obscure way that I had lost that round. "Because I wasn't planning to volunteer anyway."

"No," he said, and paused. "But *I* might have."

I paused too. The pang resumed its scurrying inside me, like an agitated small animal in a cage.

"Luckily," I said, picking my empty cup from the floor and peering into it, "I'm in no urgent need of a back rub tonight."

"Oh," he said, "I think you are." We looked into each other's eyes again, much longer than etiquette allowed, and again I was the first to break the gaze.

He was right. It had been quite a while—six months at least. Six months since Andreas, who had left me, like a burn victim, first flayed then scarred.

I thought it over for about thirty seconds. What did I have to lose? This one—what was his name, Scott—was too young to take seriously, twenty-five or -six, I guessed, while I was pushing thirty-eight; drunk, like me; willing and, I hoped, able. It might be an entertaining way to start the new year.

"THAT WAS FUN," I said, some hours later, pushing my damp hair from my face, "but now I think it might be time for you to leave."

"Now?" he asked, propping himself, rumpled and blurry, on one elbow to read the clock. "Now? At eight A.M.? On New Year's Day?"

"Sorry," I said, meaning it. "I told you I couldn't sleep with a stranger next to me. And now I need some sleep."

"Yeah," he muttered, dropping onto both elbows, face-down, and rubbing his raspy hair as if to get the circulation going in his brain, "you warned me, but I guess I didn't pay too much attention at the time."

I wriggled closer to kiss his left nipple, the only

spot I could reach. He inhaled sharply and reached for me.

"Not again," I said, rolling from his grasp. "I can't. You've done me in."

"OK," he said, and then, after a pause, nonchalant: "Do I get to come back?"

"Don't know," I said. "Probably not."

He nodded, made a wry mouth.

"No reflection on you," I added. "I had a great time."

I'd known we'd be good together. I'd felt it the moment he touched me on Angelica's sage-green sofa.

When we'd stumbled back from the party, we hadn't, at first, even made it up the stairs. On the third-floor landing, he'd pressed me against the wall and kissed me until—perhaps I was still drunk—I thought I might faint; I'd unzipped his jeans; he'd pushed up my skirt; and there, with the stucco cold and rough against my backside, we'd fucked. Then I'd led him upstairs and the night began.

Not my usual style, but, as you will recall, it was New Year's Eve, I was drunk, thirty-eight, and alone.

"I know you did," he said, sounding smug. "Or it certainly sounded like it, anyway."

I liked the way that, once dismissed, he didn't argue or cajole, just clambered out of bed with a faint hangoverish groan, fumbled for his boxer shorts, which he found down one leg of his jeans, put them on, and sank back on the bed, as if to recuperate. Without opening my eyes, I caressed his smooth, taut back.

"Nice," I said, lazily.

"Why don't I leave you my number anyway," he said. "Even though I know you won't call."

I shrugged. There was, I knew, nowhere for this encounter to go.

After a while he rose and jotted something on the pad next to the phone, then, with a jangling of pocket change, pulled on his jeans. He suddenly looked much younger and more naked, the planes of his torso clean and tight and curved. I was seized by an urge to run my hands all over him again, to lick him, but I refrained.

He shrugged on his T-shirt and leather jacket, then stuffed on his boots, leaving them unlaced. At the doorway he turned and said, "Happy New Year, Chris."

"It has been so far," I told him and he left, pausing at the top of the stairs to light, I assumed, a cigarette.

When I heard the downstairs door slam, I climbed out of bed, needing to pee. My head felt as if a large ball bearing were rolling around inside it, and my hair, I noted in the bathroom mirror, was sticking out in a strange teased mass like an aborted beehive. The skin around my mouth and chin was a flaming, tender red: his stubble had sandpapered me and I knew that by tomorrow it would begin to crack and peel.

I went back to bed as I was—gamy, unwashed—and flipped around for a while in exhausted exhilarated erotic overdrive. Then I staggered out of bed again, pulled down the shades against the sharp winter light, and slept.

TWICE A WEEK she drives from Boston to visit me here, my lawyer, each time in a different rented car, parking each time at a different spot along the road, clotting her spike heels with fibrous clumps of mud to reach my door. Sometimes she asks for clarification or further detail; today, she wants more details about the sex. Laurie, I say, I'm shocked; this is supposed to be a legal document, isn't it, not a work of pornography. Nonetheless, she insists. She insists that I establish whether or not my sexual relations with the complainant were, as she puts it, "deviant" from the start.

I don't have the energy right now to embark on a debate about sexual nomenclature, so let me just specify, for the record: the complainant and I made love several times that night—loudly, lustily, gleefully, creatively, even tenderly—but our lovemaking was not "deviant," if by that she means sadomasochistic, which, under the circumstances, she probably does. No more so, anyway, than whenever one large hard body engorged with blood penetrates another smaller, softer one, equally engorged with blood.

"FURY" SEEKS PRETRIAL SECLUSION
AP, January 15, 1995

BOSTON—Laurie Katz, flamboyant feminist lawyer for the so-called "Boston Fury," Christine Chandler, announced today that her client has gone into hiding to recover from her ordeal and to prepare for her trial.

"We've had to take this step," Ms. Katz stated, "in response to the unprecedented media frenzy that this case has generated and in response to numerous ugly threats on my client's life and well-being, many of them publicly incited over talk radio. My client will remain in seclusion until pretrial hearings begin. No further information on her whereabouts will be available until then."

Chandler, 38, a Boston attorney whose alleged brutal assault on her former lover, 25-year-old Scott DeSalvo, drew national outrage and earned her the talk-show sobriquet "Boston Fury," was released last November on $750,000 bail and remanded to a Boston-area hospital for psychiatric evaluation.

News that Chandler, pronounced fit to stand trial, had been released from the high-security ward at McLean Hospital sparked protest throughout the region this week. In Boston, thirteen demonstrators from the self-styled "JM2" Commando (Justice for Men Too) were arrested late Thursday after throwing buckets of what appeared to be animal blood on the steps of the Massachusetts State House.

"If a man had done that to a woman," JM2 leader Karl Budd told reporters, "what she did to him, there's no way he'd be walking the streets again. All we want is justice for males too."

Chandler's trial is not expected to begin for several months, according to Massachusetts Attorney General Ed O'Donoghue. "I'm not in a position to give an exact date," he said yesterday from his office, "but the taxpayers of Massachusetts may rest assured that Ms. Chandler will be brought to a speedy trial. Until justice is done, this heinous act will haunt us all."

I don't remember why I called him the next day. Or the day after that, whenever it was. Let's just say it was a whim. Or Seasonal Affective Disorder, also known as SAD. I'd been on the phone anyway— Julie had called, she was back from Rome—and the notepad caught my eye, with its huge childlike scrawl. *Scott,* it said, then his number and *Call Me!* (underlined twice). So, with the night's pleasure still lingering as a kind of radioactive half-life in my blood, I did.

"Hello," his voice crackled, causing a miniature upheaval somewhere below my ribs. "If you'd like to leave a message for Scott or for Patty, please wait for the beep." Scrabble scrabble scrabble of empty tape. *Beep.*

I immediately hung up, then, before the desolation could kick in, dialed again, composing, in a surge of Schadenfreude, an appropriately debonair message to leave on the machine. Something Patty might enjoy. Something casual. Witty. Sexy. Brief. The verbal equivalent of a pair of black bicycle shorts.

But he picked up right away, upon hearing my name.

"Chris!" he said.

"Scott," I replied.

"Great to hear from you."

"Just thought I'd check in with you." I paused. "And Patty."

"Oh," he said, mumbling. "Well. It's kind of complicated. We live together, sort of, except that, right now, she's living in Seoul. For her job."

So much the better. All I wanted was a little fling, something to get me through a few weeks of the winter, to thaw out the numbness and to crack the thin ice that was forming over my skin.

We met for Sechuan food in Somerville, at a dingy, cavernous place—my idea, well out of the way. He was already there when I arrived, slouching and smoking in the murky red bar. At first he pretended not to see me but then, as I crossed the room, he glanced up and cracked a bright sheepish grin. Clean-shaven, he looked much better than I recalled—in my mind he'd dwindled since New Year to a troglodyte of sorts—and I felt a twinge, something squirmy in the solar plexus. Damn, I remember thinking, this was supposed to be so simple.

He was jittery and, as we sat at the bar, downed one beer after another; when he tried to light a cigarette, his hands shook. "Let's eat," I said, thinking it might help, but when he picked up the menu, its jaunty red tassel trembled too. On impulse, I reached across the table and, setting the menu aside, clasped both his hands in mine, rubbing them until they pulsed. A shock for me, each time, rediscovering the blood-heat of another human being. I resisted the urge to suck his fingers, to push them between the buttons of my blouse. My underwear, I noticed, was already wet. Damn, I thought again, damn.

By the end of dinner it was clear that we were going to go home and fuck, so, since I'd taken a cab there, we left in his car. He drove in a reckless, show-offy way along the river, but when we got to the bridge, he had to skid to a halt: one lane was closed for repairs, brilliantly lit like a movie set, with traffic backed up at both ends. Ahead, a burly cop in a fluorescent orange vest cocked his ear to a walkie-talkie, trying to hear something over the loud harsh groan of the grading machine, over the cries of the work crew who rode it like stunt men in the hyper-white light.

Scott fretted for a while, craning to see around the car in front. He drummed his palms on the steering wheel. He flexed his foot on the brake pedal, letting the car roll forward a few feet until it nudged the car ahead, which in turn rolled forward a peevish foot or two.

"Don't," I said, taking his hand off the steering

wheel and putting it at last inside my blouse, on my bare breast. "Allow me to distract you."

He squeezed my nipple and groaned. "Distract me some more," he said, turning to look at me. "Please."

I shrugged and, meeting his gaze, undid the top button of my blouse; then, with deliberation, undid the remaining three. The blouse popped open and I shrugged it off, tossing it over my shoulder without a backwards glance. All I can say now is, I must have been drunk. Again.

At that moment, of course, the cop beckoned us on. The car began to move, gaining speed, past the summoning cop and into the single long open lane of the bridge. Naked from the waist, I leaned back against the dark plush of the seat, hands behind head, while Scott drove on, past the work crews riding high on their machines, past the duplicate cop with his duplicate GO sign on the other end, past the smudged faces in cars lined up waiting to cross, through the empty streets, and then home, home to the night ahead.

CHINA PEARL RESTAURANT
Somerville, MA
(617) 555-0713

Date of transaction: 1/5/94
Authorization number: 5234

FOOD $14.85
BAR $18.00
GRATUITY . . . . $ 4.50
TOTAL $37.35

Christine D. Chandler
AmEx 1234 456789 12345
Exp. date 10/95

SIGNATURE . . . .

THANK YOU! COME AGAIN!

The next time we met, what the hell, in a sushi bar right on Newbury Street, where a neon sign in the window gave him a blue-pink black eye, with a fugitive stripe of green across his cheek. He'd recently visited Japan, he said, and so he insisted on pouring the *sake* into my cup, keeping it constantly filled, as I was supposed to do in return. As I drank and talked, he listened, cupping his chin in his hand, tilting his head so that the lick of neon green wavered upward into his dark hair. He needed a shave. His top button was open, showing a small tangle of hair at the base of his throat. The inside of his right wrist, everted, was surprisingly delicate, indigo-veined. I stopped in mid-phrase, overpowered by the urge to reach across and trace that blue Nile, to feel, under my fingers, the pulse of his life.

BAR GENJI
NEWBURY ST.
(617) 555-1100

Date of transaction: 1/6/94
Authorization number: 0124

FOOD $25.50
BAR $49.75
GRATUITY $15.00
TOTAL $90.25

Christine D. Chandler
AmEx 1234 456789 12345
Exp. date 10/95

SIGNATURE . . . .

Surely I don't need to list all the times we saw each other after that, how many times we made love, and in what positions? It might make interesting reading but I don't see how it would help my case. Nor do I remember all the details, anyway— there was, you understand, a great deal else going on in my life at the time. I'd recently made partner in the law firm and was handling some of the bigger clients, which meant I was often at the office until nine or ten at night. I was still doing *pro bono* work for the Haitian project. I played squash at the club three times a week or worked out at the gym. I went to the movies, saw friends, went to the theater, bought books and clothes. But there's no point in denying that, yes, I did see him fairly often during the months of January and February, and, yes, on those occasions I did admit him, voluntarily, to my apartment. Why shouldn't I? I certainly had no desire to drive to his place, in the dubious warehousey part of the South End, and hang out in some grungy loft filled with another woman's stuff.

So, yes, he usually came to my place, we usually stayed in, opened a bottle of wine or smoked a joint, and made love. Had sex, whatever you want to call it. Sometimes we lit a fire in my fireplace, which I otherwise rarely used: I remember how hot it felt on my bare flanks; I remember how his charged hair crackled when I touched it, and how, every now and then, the logs would give a soft settling sigh. Then, at three or four A.M., he would leave.

The arrangement suited both of us, I thought, since I was preoccupied with work and he was, as you may recall, living with someone who, on a mere technicality, lived in Seoul. True, we didn't discuss that situation much at first—as far as I was concerned, it was his problem, not mine. But I do want to emphasize that, contrary to what some of the papers have reported, I was *not* seeing other men at the time—certainly not the "stable" of young men that's been attributed to me. If my situation weren't so dire, I'd want to burst out laughing. Where would I have found them? Where, more to the point, would I have found the time? The simple truth is that, like most of the professional women I know, I spent most of my time alone.

INT. NIGHT. LONG SHOT, DIMLY LIT HALLWAY. WOMAN WITH BRIEFCASE unlocks apartment door, drops mail on hall table, pushes each shoe off with the other foot, puts briefcase down on chair, unbuttons coat, unwinds scarf, holding it in place with chin, and then hangs coat and scarf, scarf first, on hook behind the door. TRACKING SHOT down hallway into living room as she turns up thermostat, switches on TV, pads into kitchen, opens refrigerator, pours herself a glass of juice, replaces carton in near-empty refrigerator. CLOSE-UP on carton of calcium-enriched orange juice. TRACKING SHOT from kitchen to desk, where WOMAN checks answering machine. Abbreviated SQUEAL of blank tape.

Last year, in one of my periodic funks about the futility of human existence, particularly my own, I'd imagined someone secretly videotaping my life and showing this little coming-home sequence, endlessly repeated, as evidence of my pointless sojourn on the planet. So, for a week or so, I'd tried to do things differently. I'd scheduled a little spontaneity into my life. But then I discovered there was a logic to the way I already did things: if I put my briefcase down before kicking off my shoes, for instance, I'd only track slush further into the house, and so on. So I'd returned to my rituals. They were, after all, the only ones I had.

MY LAWYER HAS asked me for the names of witnesses she could depose, friends or co-workers who might be willing to testify to the nature of the relationship in its initial stages. What, I ask her, startled, you mean someone who *watched?* No of course not, she replies, equally startled, I mean someone with whom you discussed the relationship.

Someone with whom I discussed the relationship? I ask dubiously. No-one, of course. Well, Angelica, I guess. Sort of.

I'D RUN INTO her on Newbury Street one Saturday afternoon—I was on my way to the hairdresser, she was shopping for shoes—and she'd intercepted me by planting herself a few yards ahead of me on the icy sidewalk, so that, barreling along with my head down, I almost crashed into her.

"Chris," she'd said, kissing me. "You should look where you're going. And what an evil glare you gave me, girl! How've you been?"

"Busy," I'd replied, grinning and wiping a smear of Viva Glam from my cheek. "Distracted. As you can see."

It was, we agreed, too chilly to linger outside, so we stepped into a nearby café, where the air was soft and steamy and cinnamon-scented.

"Over there," she pointed, finding the only free table, wriggling into it, and dumping someone's abandoned newspaper on the floor. She took off her funky velvet hat but left her dark glasses on, a habit that irritated me: I like to see someone's eyes when we're talking, not the tiny gaping goldfish of my own reflection.

"It's been a while, hasn't it?" I said, meaning since last I'd seen her, which had been New Year's Eve. "I keep planning to stop in for a drink on my way home, but by the time I leave the office these days I'm usually too beat." Angelica tended bar downtown three nights a week, and I liked to watch her in action, dominatrix of her black marble domain.

"Not too beat, I hear, to keep up with twenty-five-year-old boys," she said, leaning back with a lush creamy lipsticked smile. Cannily watching my face, she lit a cigarette.

"He's twenty-seven, nearly twenty-eight," I lied. "And anyway, it's nothing, just sex."

"Great," she said, never averse to the idea of sex as a guiding principle in human conduct. "Just what you need. Especially after that weird Andreas thing." Then, catching the waiter's eye, she ordered a double espresso for her, decaf for me.

"It *is* just what I need," I agreed, as he left. "Something fun. Manageable. On my terms, for a change."

She smiled again but, because of her dark glasses, I couldn't tell whether it was at me or at the appealing but underaged bicycle messenger we'd both noticed at the next table.

"Angelica," I said, pointing to her eyes, "there's not a whole lot of sun in here. Why don't you take those damn things off?"

"Because," she said, removing them and laying them carefully on the tablecloth, two wire-rimmed discs of beer-bottle green. She tilted her face, without expression, towards me. Beneath one eye, like eyeshadow applied with a careless hand, was a delicate swath of indigo, shading into violet, teal, and the faintest tinge of buttercup.

An incredulous thrill went through me. "Bruce?" I asked.

She shrugged.

"You must be out of your fucking mind," I said. "You could have any man you wanted. Or woman." And it was true: with her husky laugh, her tulip-red lips, and her lithe, rounded puppy-body, which she displayed to good effect, Angelica could have anyone she wanted—and usually did.

"It's only when he does too much blow," she said, shrugging again and letting out a last big blue smoky lungful before stubbing out the butt.

WHAT ABOUT JULIE, my lawyer asks? Or Stephanie? Shouldn't she depose them too? Well, yes, I tell her,

you could depose them; I had them both over for
dinner in January, I believe, soon after Julie arrived
back in town. But if memory serves—which it
seems increasingly reluctant to do—I didn't mention Scott at all, probably because he played, at
the time, such a bit part in my life. Mentioning
him would also have violated the unwritten rule
of my evenings with Stephanie and Julie, which for
some time now had been largely devoted to be-
moaning the fact that we never got laid. Also, to be
frank, I suppose I was a little afraid of Julie's dis-
dain.

"A twenty-four-year-old, what, boy-toy?" I could
imagine her saying, frighteningly chic in her new
Parisian buzz-cut. "What on earth do you talk
about?"

(The answer, by the way, would have been
(a) ourselves and (b) our sexual transactions. Occasionally, in passing, I would explain to him who
Twyla Tharp was, or Philip Glass, and he would fill
me in on, say, Courtney Love. But mostly we stuck
with (a) and (b) and did all right.)

All I really remember from that dinner is, as
usual, how tired we all were. By the time we'd
killed a bottle of Moët—Julie's gift from the duty-
free—followed by my more modest Merlot with din-

ner, we'd each sunk into our own version of torpor. Steph's face had petrified into a polite but vacant smile while she thought about something else—viruses, I guessed, or pigs; I was chewing my cuticles and wondering what to wear to work the next day; and Julie kept lifting her glass to the light, swirling it, putting it down, then swirling it again.

By this stage of the evening, the track lighting above the table had become downright unkind, picking out each pore in our late-night faces. Julie, the thin one, looked haggard, with an oily sheen on her sharp nose and a tracework of fine lines around her eyes. Stephanie, the plump one, looked puffy, as if she'd been on an eating binge for a week, which, come to think of it, she probably had. As for me, I knew only too well what long hours and overhead lighting could do to my looks, especially where gravity was working on the mouth.

The table was cluttered with unwashed dishes, the pots in the kitchen were bilious with pesto, and I just wanted everyone to leave so I could start cleaning up. I'd heard enough by now about Julie's sabbatical, and more than enough about her culture shock on returning, her sudden discovery that the women in this country have no style and the coffee is undrinkable. All of this delivered to Stephanie and me—Steph admittedly wearing sweatpants—over a cup of my water-process decaf.

"So," she asked, as an afterthought, "what's been happening with you guys?"

"Oh nothing," I said, trying to think of something. "The usual."

There must have been something. Work, of course: the final phases of a tricky case that had dragged on for two years. A conference deadline. A distant cousin in a coma. The condo, of course, but we're not allowed to mention that in front of Julie, who makes a big show of glazing over when Stephanie and I talk property. As I said, I didn't think to mention Scott.

"Well," said Stephanie, braving the taboo, "I had a skylight put in the upstairs bedroom."

Julie made the predictable grimace. She doesn't even know she's doing it anymore: it's what psychologists call a micro-gesture. Steph met my eyes and made her own micro-gesture, somewhere between a smile and a shrug, something that said "That's life," or "That's Julie," or "What can you do?"

"And there was this really cute carpenter who came to work on my house . . ." Steph said, making a Betty Boop face, as if telling a naughty joke (the one about the carpenter who went to put a window in the lady's bedroom). That's all she said, and I knew she'd never tell Julie the rest, nor that she was still pursuing him through small-claims court for the five hundred dollars he'd bilked her of.

I wasn't going to tell Julie about Andreas either. That was too recent, too raw, and the ridiculously expensive birthday-dinner dress reproached me every time I opened the closet, a slinky black skin with the price tag still attached.

"Aren't you exhausted?" I asked Julie, hopefully. "Jet lag catching up with you yet?"

"Actually, no," she said. "I'm starting to perk up again because it's, what, about seven in the morning biological time."

Steph yawned and rubbed her temples, as if her braided red hair were beginning to itch. I knew she'd been having a rough time at the lab lately—company politics, pitting her against the immunologists who infected pigs with the viruses she engineered—and needed to go home.

"Well," I said, brushing baguette crumbs into a cupped hand, "I'm on Boston time and I have an eight-thirty tomorrow."

Steph pushed her chair back and squeezed out, paroled at last. From where she stood, she started piling up plates.

"Oh don't bother," I said. "I'll do it later."

"Thanks for cooking," said Julie, who never did. She gestured vaguely at the wreckage and then began gathering up her belongings, the new black briefcase from Paris, the jacket from Milan. There'd been a time, not so long ago, when she'd worn nothing but blue jeans and men's jackets from the thrift store. She'd said, then, that it was a matter of principle.

"Don't forget your photos," I reminded her, "they're on the coffee table."

At the doorway, I gave them each a quick hug, a task I never enjoyed because Julie felt like a sea urchin, so sharp and frail, while Steph's bluff, bulky embrace never failed to knock the breath out of me and leave me coated in dog hair. As the door clicked shut behind them, I reached for the lint brush. People were always asking me why I didn't get a cat: I'd say I couldn't handle the commitment, but the truth was I couldn't handle the hair.

My contact lenses felt dry and scratchy, so I took them out and cleaned them, halfheartedly, half-ass. Then I brushed back my hair and pushed on a headband to keep it out of the way while I washed my face. The headband was too tight, so it rode slowly backwards and upwards, pushing a thick reddish-brown frizz behind it, a slow-motion finger-in-the-socket effect. Exposed, my forehead was scored across with lines whose origins I still don't understand. Are my eyebrows really riding up and down like that all the time? Wouldn't I know?

Mirrors, I remembered reading somewhere, are the doors through which death enters the world.

TO: Laurie
FROM: Felice
RE: Chandler defense

Here's the excerpt you asked me to prepare from the Duverger deposition. I'm not sure how helpful it will be—you'll see why—but here it is anyway. I tried to cut out all the stuff you already know. Fax me back if you need more.

DEPOSITION OF JULIE CLAIRE DUVERGER, Ph.D.
Associate Professor, Department of Romance Languages
Boston University
January 23, 1995

Sure, I'll give it a shot, but I really don't think there's too much I can tell you. For one thing, I never met this Scott character, and, for another, there was just so much going on in my life at the time. I'd just come back from six months in Europe, so I was completely overwhelmed by

being back in Boston, by the greyness of it all,
you know, the bleakness. Everything looked so
ugly—everything—the buildings, the billboards,
the trash on the streets, the *people*—well, I just
went into a kind of depression for a few
months and didn't really notice much that was
going on around me.

Then I got involved with this guy in New
York—what a loser, but that's another story—
so I was gone a lot in the spring and, I don't
know, with work and all, I really didn't see
much of Chris. And then I left in June again,
because I never stay in Boston over the
summer: it's unlivable, people start going a
little bit crazy without realizing what's
happening to them.

My point? Well, my point is, I didn't really
know what was happening with Chris: I didn't
even know she was involved with anyone—I
thought she still had a thing for that actor guy,
what was his name, André—because Chris
would never tell you anything. Anything
personal, I mean. You had to pry and pry. I
can be a little reticent myself sometimes, sure,
but with Chris, well, you needed the electric
can-opener.

Sorry. OK. I'll try to stick to the point. Well,
anyway, Chris would never tell you anything,
but usually, as far as I could see, that was
because there wasn't that much to tell. She'd
go to work, come home, go to the gym, play
squash, whatever. Get back around nine-thirty,
take a shower, go to sleep by eleven, very

rigid routine, whereas I'm much more
spontaneous, more of a night person.

OK, I'm getting to that. All I remember—and
I've racked my brains since this terrible thing
happened, believe me—is that I took a bottle
of Veuve Cliquot over there soon after I got
back—so that would've been the beginning of
the year, right? But I was in such a fog, from
the jet lag and, I suppose, some kind of reverse
culture shock, that I wasn't really tuned in to
my surroundings. And also when you've been
away for a while, it can take you some time to
get back in synch with your friends, I don't
know if you've noticed this.

Chris cooked, I remember, nothing special,
and was being obsessive-compulsive about
cleaning up, the way she always is. Steph was
there too—are you going to speak to Steph,
Steph Ryan?—and they both seemed to be
having a good time, looking at my photos,
laughing at my stories and so on. A little
envious, perhaps, because they'd been stuck in
Boston while I'd been in Paris and Milan, but
that's only natural, isn't it.

Chris can be really good company when she
puts her mind to it, you know. Funny. Quick.
Good listener. That's how I remember her that
night.

I wish there was more I could tell you, but
really, it was just such a hectic time for me.

One of the few advantages of living in New England is that it has weather, serious weather, which

makes it easier to place recollected events in time.
Today, for instance, the sky is dense and milky, like
ouzo, with, in the distance, three horses huddled
against a penciled-in fence. So in my mind, it will
always be winter here, winter in Vermont, winter
like a hangover, hopeless and bleached. Winter in
Steph's cabin, fifteen miles from Peacham, Vermont, pop.—these days—301.

To resume, however: one of the advantages of
New England, from the mnemonic point of view, is
that it has weather. Unlike memories from, say,
California or Mexico or Greece, which come tinted
a uniform sparkling blue, each memory from New
England has its own light, its own color, its own
degree of clemency on the skin. That's how I know
that, contrary to absurd allegations that I took him
to Disney World and bought him a Bambi mug, or
some such nonsense, the complainant and I never
spent more than a few consecutive hours together
until the spring—the beginning of spring. Then,
yes, we went away for a weekend in the country: I
can still smell the savor of the grass.

It was my idea—a whim, really—and he was
happy, no, make that delighted, to go along with it.
I told him I knew the perfect place (from, I didn't
tell him, a champagne-fueled night with Andreas)

and as the car crunched up the long curved drive-way, it did look idyllic: a sprawling inn in the foot-hills of the Berkshires, with a few smaller cottages scattered about the grounds.

"Wow," he said. "Check this out."

As I climbed out and stretched, the soft air nuzzled my face, bringing with it a hint of new grass.

"Oh," I said, "smell that, Scott. Spring."

Sniffing—which he tended to do anyway: damaged septum—and smiling as if he were personally responsible, as if he had planned this green scent for me like a young Chardonnay, he draped his arm over my shoulders and, looped lazily together, we strolled inside.

"Miss Chandler," said the pink-and-white lady behind the desk, finding my reservation, "you're in luck. I can give you one of the cottages this time." It was tiny and self-contained like a dolls' house, complete with its own little porch; inside, in the inimitable style of New England inns, it was ruffled and ruched on every plane surface. A huge canopied bed occupied most of the room, but, daunted by that lacy pillowed nest, we immediately made love on the floor. A braided rag rug, I discovered—in hindsight—can cause a spectacular case of rug burn.

I took a long, languid shower while he opened a

bottle of Cabernet that had been waiting, with two unripe pears, next to the bed. "For you, babe," he said, bringing a glass into the bathroom and returning to the other room, where a sudden loud blast of static told me he'd switched on the TV. About fifteen minutes later, when I stepped out of the shower, I caught a glimpse of him through the open door. Naked, with his hair awry and his cheeks still flushed, he looked, for a second, like someone I had never seen. Someone male and willful, a big sullen child. There was a naked body in the room, I realized, a big naked child, and I hadn't the slightest idea who he was.

This is, I hope you will agree, the kind of moment that can occur between any two people in a hotel room—hell, between two people who've been married for years. One person looks at the other and, in a moment of awful spiraling vertigo, feels that she has never seen that face before. My parents' marriage, for instance, seems no more—or less—weary, stale, flat, and unprofitable than anyone else's, but when I see them in the connubial bed, what I really want to know is, *Haven't you ever woken up and realized that there's a foreign body lying next to you? Haven't you ever wondered, with dread, how it got there?*

To quell the slight fizz of fear—nothing major—I turned to stare at my own face in the glass. It looked, I thought, like me: hazel eyes gold-flecked like a cat's, full lips, good bones; I'd make a handsome old crone some day. Exhaling, I combed out my wet hair and then, since I had the time, plugged in the hair dryer from my travel kit. It blasted out hot air for a few seconds and suddenly, without warning, metamorphosed into a miniature flame-thrower, emitting loud bright crackling blue and orange sparks, bright enough to illuminate the bathroom in flashes, like fireworks.

I noted, as if in a freeze-frame, how my fingers tightened instead of letting go, and then, with a loud panicky "Aahh," I hurled the treacherous thing to the floor, where it continued to flame and sputter. When at last I found the presence of mind to yank the plug out of the wall, it sizzled cobalt and died, leaving a burnt sulfurous whiff on the air. I stood naked and trembling, staring at the appliance on the aqua bathmat as if it might next begin speaking in tongues. My palm, I realized, was tingling, and, turning it towards me, I saw that the joint between thumb and finger had been branded. I bore, like a sign, a small crescent of powdery black.

Through the open door, I saw Scott exactly as he

had been, eyes fixed on the TV, finger playing restlessly over the remote control. Wrapping a towel around me and extending my branded hand like a hysteric, I walked towards the bed.

"So what was that all about?" he asked, still focused on the screen.

"What was what all about?"

"The sparks, the noise, everything."

"You saw that?"

He hit the remote and the game came on. Trying, through the roar and confusion, to deduce the score, he didn't respond.

"But then," I asked, "why didn't you do anything?"

"What?"

"Why didn't you do anything?"

"About what?"

"About the fact that I was practically being electrocuted before your eyes."

"Is that what was happening?" he asked, turning for the first time to look at me. "Are you OK?"

I held out my hand, with its matte black mark. I still couldn't keep it from trembling.

"Poor baby," he said, and pressed it to his lips.

"Asshole," I said, in a wave of sick disbelief.

"Hey," he said, "I said, poor baby." He kissed

my hand again, with an exaggerated smack. "Poor burnt baby. All better now?"

"Asshole," I repeated and went back into the bathroom, busying myself with my toilette for a long, long time. Who'd have paid the bill if he'd had to call the chambermaid to sweep me, a dust-pan-full of ash, off the marbled tiles, I wanted to ask. Who'd have paid the bill if I'd been fried?

Nevertheless, I didn't make too much of it at the time: it seemed, as I have said, the kind of odd moment, missed connection, that might occur between any two strangers in a hotel room—another reason that, before and since Andreas, I've avoided close quarters, the morning after, enforced intimacy of any kind. (There was Tom, of course, but we never shared a bedroom, rarely a bed.)

Nor did I make much of it later when, while we were writhing on the rug again, he rolled his entire weight onto me, and—as he'd done before, making me squirm and whimper with delight—grasped my hair and twisted my head to bite my nape. This time, though, his elbow ended up against my throat, poking into my windpipe for a few sharp seconds. I gagged and thrashed, he noticed, and, with a little grunt, as if of apology, he moved his elbow away.

Such accidents are inevitable, I believe, when

two foreign bodies flail blindly against each other, trying to find, in the parlance of the massage parlor, relief.

In other words: *safe sex:* an oxymoron if ever I heard one.

And why deny, anyway, that this was part of the kick of it, part of the edge: that if I opened my eyes and looked into his candid young face, racked with pleasure, I could savor the sharp thrill of transgression; but if I closed them and concentrated on the body pinning me down, the weight, the density of it, the power of its blunt heavy limbs, I'd know, too, that he was a man and could really hurt me.

HAMPTON MANOR
Stockbridge, Mass.

Date of transaction: 4/10/94
Authorization number: 2538

Your Visit: 4/9/94–4/10/94
RM (ROSE COTTAGE)
@ $350 .... $350.00
RM SVCE (BAR) $120.00
RM SVCE (BRNCH)........ $82.79
MASSAGE (2 PERS) $130.00
TOTAL (TX INCL) $682.79

Guest
Christine D. Chandler

AmEx 1234 456789 12345
Exp. date 10/95

We Appreciate Your Patronage . . .

My lawyer says I should erase that last paragraph and move this document along, but I don't know what else to include. My life, until that one moment—bathed in red from the Sheraton sign—was bloodless, predictable, public-spirited. Every day I went in to a sealed glass tower at the heart of the financial district, rode up to the eleventh floor, and dealt with piles of paper covered with little black marks and lines and squares. Every day I dealt with human beings who for some reason wanted to be *here* on the planet rather than *there*. Every day I heard the same questions in different accents and most days I gave the same replies. Some days I did paperwork for plastic surgeons and software engineers. Other days I took down stories of torture, war, women gang-raped at bayonet point, children ripped apart by bullets on their way to school. Every day Rosa, my paralegal, showed up in her skirted suit and cowboy boots, read our horoscopes from the tabloid paper, and, on her way to the deli downstairs, asked me if I wanted anything from the world—a question I never knew how to answer.

* * *

THROUGH THE MONTH of April—chilled blue air in the city, a few misguided magnolias beginning to bud—the complainant and I continued to see each other, and have carnal knowledge of each other, every ten days or so. He may occasionally have expressed a desire for more—more time together, more carnal knowledge; it's possible, I'm not denying it. If he had, though, I probably would have mentioned Patty, and that would have been the end of the discussion. Whenever her name came up, which wasn't often, he'd grimace, eyes downcast, mouth stretched into a tight shamed line. He hadn't told her yet, of course. Later he did—but I'll get to that.

I don't mean to sound callous, you understand, but the terms of our contract were, I believed, clear from the outset. He was the one who was living with someone else, after all, in a kind of late-twentieth-century virtual geography. And, besides, I had nothing more to give: my thirty-eight years had left me as brittle and empty as a horseshoe crab desiccating on the beach.

Nor do I mean to imply that there wasn't affection, playfulness, even tenderness between us. Conversation, too, of a sort. Obviously there was, otherwise we wouldn't have bothered. Or I wouldn't have; I can't speak for him. I remember a moment from, oh it must have been February, or maybe even March, when we lay naked before the fire, and for the first time he really looked at me. Until then he'd kept his eyes clenched shut while we had sex, as if monitoring some distant internal pain, but this time he pushed me back against the Bokhara and looked at me, really looked, tracing with his fingertips the contours of my face and neck: cheekbones, collarbones, eyelids, lips. For a while I kept my own eyes closed but then, I don't know why, opened them and looked back. His gaze burnt a clear path to some deep center of my brain, which, astonished, responded by inundating me with feeling, a violent visceral sensation somewhere between soaring and free-fall.

HAVE I DESCRIBED him yet, blue-green-grey eyes, depending on his mood and the color of his clothes, smooth taut skin, not much body hair, broad shoulders, small but nicely defined muscles in his arms, strong calves, tight wiry tendons behind his knees? Have I described how he smelt, of leather and cigarettes and darkroom chemicals? Have I described the odd things he would do sometimes, like take the boiling kettle from the stove, pour the water into the teapot, and then, without thinking, stow the kettle in the fridge? Have I described how he took his solid young body for granted, neglecting it, abusing it, pushing it too far—as if it would last forever, as if nothing or no-one could ever harm it?

IT WAS IN April, too, or maybe the beginning of May, that I felt the first inklings of a flight response. I'd known from the start that the situation, in its un-complicated form, had a finite life span, so it didn't surprise me when I began to see signs of mutation. Small signs, at first—like Angelica's mentioning, by the way, that Scott had stopped by the bar a few nights earlier with, as she put it, "some babe from *Things*." (She mentioned it, of course, thinking that I wouldn't care, not that I would—that's not Angel-ica's style.) But I did care, not about the babe, you understand—she was within the terms of the im-plied contract—but about the bar: Angelica's bar, too close to home. Too calculated. Nor did I care for the stab of dismay that went through me at the news.

The next incident, frankly, I find a little embarrassing to describe. Oh, you may laugh up your nice clean sleeve at the idea that I'd find anything embarrassing after what I've already described to the police, but, yes, it embarrasses me; it embarrasses me to dredge up these memories, these minutiae, for strangers to pore over. It embarrasses me the way admitting a stupid error at work might embarrass someone else. I prefer to make my mistakes in private. *Preferred.*

So I'll be brief. If the purpose of this document is to help establish guilt or innocence, then, in this sole instance, I'll admit guilt. For breaking the rules. Or, at least, for changing them.

I'd been to a conference in D.C.—something to do with political asylum, I forget what, perhaps Laurie's intern can look it up for me—and, to get to the point, by the third day I was bored. Bored with the presentations, bored with the long grim cocktail hours, bored in my refrigerated hotel room with CNN for company. And, why deny it, I had been thinking of him, the way that, alone in a hotel room, one yearns for another human body, warm and damp and salty, to help derange the sheets. So I called up the airline and, sacrificing some of my frequent-flyer miles, rescheduled my flight. Within hours, I was stepping out of terminal B into the breezy Boston night.

Redeeming my car from the airport lot, I felt—perhaps for the first time in my life—anonymous and free. Nobody in the world knew where I was: Rosa wasn't expecting me back at the office for two days, and if a colleague should call the hotel, he'd find I'd checked out. I could do anything, go anywhere, but I headed for home; then, speeding through the spangled streets, I was seized by a whim.

I'd never been to his place before. Why not now? Bad idea, I knew—if I'd learned anything from Andreas, it was never to arrive unannounced. Bad idea, breaking that rule, not smart at all, but I was already in the exit lane, already negotiating the rutted streets of the South End, already checking my hair in the rearview mirror as I bumped to a halt on his block. I guessed, correctly, that a row of lit windows on the third floor was his, since, according to the buzzers in the lobby, the other two floors were occupied by a sail maker and a label-printing business.

"Yup?" came his voice when I rang, hollow and uncertain as if speaking from the bottom of a well.

"It's me," I said—unfairly, I suppose.

"Who?" he asked, after a pause.

"Chris," I said. "Surprise."

Another pause, then the front door buzzed open, admitting me to an unlit, plywood-boarded stairwell. As I began to climb, I heard his footsteps booming down to meet me. He wore ripped jeans and a sweatshirt, socks but no shoes. He looked surprised, confused, sheepish, and genuinely delighted to see me, all at the same time.

"I thought you were in D.C.," he said, pecking me on the lips and leading me up to the open door of his loft. "And I *never* thought you would show up here. Wow. Come on in."

Over his shoulder, through the entryway, I glimpsed a large studio–cum–living space, none too clean, with a thicket of exposed ducts overhead. I also noticed—in this order—a long, deeply scarred black leather sofa with, at one end, an abandoned guitar, and, at the other, bent over a second guitar, a piebald peroxide job. One thin tattooed arm.

I made a faint gargling sound and stopped.

"Come in," he repeated. "Jen's here."

"Jen?" I croaked.

"Used to be in the band with me, she's going solo now. We're working on a new song for her demo tape. Come on in and listen."

My voice returned, in an electrical surge. "I don't think so," I said. "I think I'll just go on home."

"But," he said.

When next I noticed anything, I was driving next to the river, much too fast, with the radio turned high, hammering my skull. For some reason, I was gasping—not crying, but gasping, hoarse rasping gasps on the in-breath, fighting for oxygen like a landed fish. I swung recklessly from lane to lane, lusting for a crash; for the first time I understood why so many accidents occur. Some drivers out there are just *very upset*.

MY LAWYER THINKS I should avoid mentioning this incident as well, since (a) its significance is not clear and (b) it doesn't reflect well on me. True, I tell her, but may I say, in my defense, that intimate relations don't always bring out the best in people. That's why I prefer to avoid them. *Preferred.*

Also, if I'm to limit my account to events that reflect well on me, I may as well pack it in right now. I should have packed it in before it even started, before I entered, stage left, falling-down-drunk. OK, she says, but let's try to adhere to some criterion of relevance—relevance to the charges at hand. Mayhem, and so on. I know, I say. I'm trying. But how can I be sure what's relevant if I still don't understand what happened, or why? For instance, is it relevant that, the first time we had sex, he picked my short black slip off the floor next to the bed and laid it—gently at first—over my face? That I gasped and sucked in silk, flailed, told him I could hardly breathe? That, holding the fabric in place, he fell upon me with a moan, biting my breasts until, blind and breathless, I moaned too, spiraling alone through very black space?

WHERE WAS I? Leaving his house, not paying much attention to highway safety.

OK, I thought, after that ludicrous incident, enough. This isn't fun any more. Surely I have better things to do than chase down twenty-six-year-old boys, only to find them, unsurprisingly, with twenty-six-year-old girls. I had broken the rules and now remembered why I'd made them in the first place: to avoid precisely this. This sensation of helplessness, this distracting ache.

Odd how Andreas' name keeps coming into this. I was hoping to avoid the subject of Andreas altogether, and I'm still not convinced that it's germane to the topic at hand, but the name has, I admit, recurred. So, to avoid trying your patience any further, let me briefly characterize the Andreas episode: semi-famous actor, grand passion, two years, egomaniac, broken heart. Liar, too: what did I expect?

This is, I've decided, what causes the harm: not being lied to, but the long drop of finding out, of discovering that you're the only person in the story who doesn't know the plot.

I DECIDED TO avoid Scott for the next couple of weeks, and, if memory serves, I did; I think I even recall the series of baffled then increasingly angry messages that he left on my machine at home and with Rosa at work. Nuisance caller, I called him, when she asked.

As I said, intimate relations do not always bring out the best in people.

I tried not to think about him but my body was determined to thwart me, tormenting me with desire, an ever-present itch that drove me, over the next few weeks, to unprecedented feats with domestic appliances and so on. I doubt that the details are relevant—nor what, precisely, I did behind the locked door of my office in my business suit. All I want to establish is that a little sex is a dangerous thing. When there's no sex to be had, the body accepts its lot and shuts down. When there's enough sex to be had, the body relaxes like a well-fed cat. But a little sex, punctuating a period of dearth, can send the body into a tailspin of lust.

This is, I think, what happened to me. I can think of no other explanation for my condition, in which the hot tonguing of the shower made me squirm, the cool breath of the wind under my hair made me squirm, the long tense muscles of a passing jogger's thigh made me squirm. My own touch made me squirm, as I ran my fingernails fretfully over my skin, as I sucked the flesh of my arms to feel the sting of his touch.

In other words, I suppose, I missed him. Or, at least, my body did.

Perhaps that explains what happened next. Perhaps not. I'll leave it to you to decide. And, eventually, I suppose, to the legal system—the legal system, about which I know so much, though nothing that can help me now.

* * *

WHAT HAPPENED NEXT was this, more or less. Not to put too fine a point on it, I'd gone to bed drunk, after a long evening of solitary sousing. (Yes, you can add incipient alcoholism to the charges; I'd somehow lost the knack of being alone.) The next thing I recall is something sawing through my sleep, through my skull, then sawing, loudly, again.

I was on the edge of the bed with my heart rioting before, regaining self, I identified the sound. My buzzer was ringing, in the middle of the night, no, 4:07 A.M., but pitch dark. Clutching my bathrobe around me, I went over and peered out of the front window, which offered an aerial view, spotlit and foreshortened, of the steps, the doorway, and the coif of whoever might be pressing the bell. Even without my contact lenses, I could tell it was him. He was partway down the stairs, craning his neck up at my window as if anticipating that I'd look out.

"You!" I mouthed, like someone in a melodrama.

He gestured extravagantly, making a swimming motion, like the hero bursting through the double saloon doors in a western. It meant, I gathered, "Let me in."

"No," I mouthed.

"Please," he mouthed back. "Please."

In fascist states, I've read, the security police

will come for you at four A.M., when, on a circadian scale, your resistance is feeblest, your defenses at their lowest ebb. It was now 4:11, but, biologically speaking, close enough. I buzzed him in.

In the time it took him to stomp up the stairs, I knotted the sash on my bathrobe and tugged my fingers through my tangled hair. When he reached my door, I—yes, voluntarily, again—let him in, though only as far as the hallway. He was disheveled and damp, with dark streaks under his eyes that made him look, almost, deranged. For a second I felt afraid. Then I realized that he had been drinking. *He too*, I should say.

"Chris," he asked, "what the fucking hell is going on?" Not an unreasonable question, given that I had refused to speak to him for three weeks.

I stood against the wall, arms folded shut.

"You really have a fucking nerve," he said, over-articulating his words the way he tended to when drunk. "You and your little rules, which you keep changing so that no-one except you ever knows what they are."

It was true, I realized: I and my little rules, designed to keep out the chaos. As if, I was to learn, anything could.

"I'm sick of it," he said. "It's not fair." He kicked the baseboard for emphasis, leaving a chevron-shaped smudge, and said again, "It's not fucking fair."

"True," I said. "We should talk."

"Talk!" he said. "You're the one who won't talk to me."

"Yes, talk, but not now, because it's four in the morning and I'm tired and you're drunk."

"I don't want to talk," he said. "I want to fuck you."

"Well I don't want to fuck you," I said. "Because it's four in the morning and I'm tired and you're drunk."

"No," he said, "you only want to fuck me when it suits you. When it fucking well suits *you*."

"That may be true," I said, "but you never seemed to mind before."

He seized me by the shoulders and slammed me against the wall. "Well, I mind now," he said, quietly, tightening his grip on the flesh of my upper arm. "I want to fuck you now. When it suits *me*."

"Don't be ridiculous," I said, pushing him away. "Go home and call me tomorrow."

"I won't," he said. "Don't push me like that."

"I will," I replied, "if you grab me like that." As he began to turn away, I gave him a nudge on the shoulder blade to emphasize my point.

"Stop that!" he shouted, spinning around and shoving me, hard, to the floor. On the way down, my back whacked against the wall, winding me, my skin scraped the stucco, and my head landed, with a light, festive knock, at his feet. Well, I thought, stunned, here I am on the floor. My next thought was that he was going to kick me in the face.

"Oh God," he said. "Are you OK?"

"I think so," I said, propping myself up on one palm.

"Oh God," he said, kneeling beside me and hooking his hands under my armpits to pull me up.

"Don't ever do that again," I said, unsteadily. I swayed on my feet, crooked an elbow, and twisted my neck to see the back of that arm, where the skin was scraped off.

"I won't," he said, his eyes filling with tears. "Oh God."

My eyes filled too.

"Oh, Chris," he said. "I just don't know what to do." He grasped me and pressed my face into his chest, into his neck, into the salty dry-biscuity scent of him. A hot dark wave of sensation flooded me, dizzying me, and I clutched him back. He picked me up and, staggering only a little under my weight, carried me to the bed where, as the street-cleaning machines began rumbling and swishing below, and the day began to break, we made love as never before.

MY LAWYER—SHE of the spike heels and the telegenic haircut, she of the yellow linen suit—my lawyer has asked me to define *push, nudge,* and *shove.* Next, I suppose, she's going to ask me to define *sensation:* which, precisely, and where? If I knew that, if I had known that then, I wouldn't be where I am now—still dangerously at a loss for definitions.

2

The next morning he dressed and left immediately, muttering something about not wanting to get a parking ticket. That may strike you as an unsatisfactory aubade, but then you probably aren't familiar with the rapacity of the meter maids on Commonwealth Avenue. Anyway, I was glad to see him go, glad to have time to reconstitute myself; I felt weak and febrile, aching all over as if I were ill.

I called Rosa to say I would be late, sat back at the kitchen table, winced, and poured myself a third cup of Sumatra, hoping it would shock my brain cells alive. Reaching for the cream, I blindsided the carton instead, spilling a few splotches, lumpy and sour. "Damn," I said, to no-one in particular, and mopped up the mess with a credit-card slip. The day was already too much for me, and it hadn't begun.

I also knew, then, that I was in this alone. I'd known it from the moment I'd opened my eyes, sensing that, behind a thin red scrim of sleep, I'd been awake for a while. I was in this alone, I understood—in this, with him, alone.

From the moment my back had whacked against the wall, from the moment my head had hit the floor, I'd entered into a zone I couldn't yet name. A zone where it seemed possible, by a single act of will, to leave will behind; to cede, at last, the dead weight of the self. A zone where someone else would take on the hard labor of being me, of deciding, every second, how to deploy body and mind. I can't tell you what a surprise it was to find myself there, nor— though I probably shouldn't admit this—what a relief. My mind went down without a struggle, into the whirlpool, into the dark; my senses found black space and shattered like a meteor shower.

My lawyer says she has no idea what I'm talking about. I shouldn't expect her to, I suppose, but I wish, sometimes, that she would.

SHOCKING NEW REVELATIONS IN "FURY" CASE! LAWYER'S SECRET PLEASURE DUNGEON: EXCLUSIVE PICS, PAGE 3
The National Investigator, November 22, 1994

Christine Chandler, the so-called "Boston Fury," entertained her boy-toys with an arsenal of sex toys in a game that spun dangerously out of control, investigators say. A search of Chandler's Back Bay penthouse unveiled the trappings of the Harvard-trained lawyer's secret life—handcuffs, blindfolds, and other bondage devices, along with large quantities of marijuana and booze. "I'm not at liberty to describe everything we saw there," an informed source said, "but, let me just tell you, it's not what you'd expect to find in the average lawyer's bedside table." Chandler's kinky relationship with 24-year-old hunk Scott DeSalvo hit the skids last October, culminating in a gruesome act of violence that shocked the entire nation. During a drunken lovers' tryst, or an S&M session gone horribly wrong, Chandler, 39, assaulted the budding photographer with her bare hands, (continued on p. 3)

So, NO, WE didn't review our situation that morning, but a day or two later, over dinner and a couple of bottles of wine, we did. At that time, as I recall, we renegotiated the terms of our contract, with particular reference to Patty.

On the subject of Patty, I wish to clear up an annoying misconception that, in the tabloids at least, has taken on a life of its own. Looking for an "angle," the media have decided to portray me as an aging workaholic, goaded, I suppose, by loneli-

PIA MATTSSON
EXT. 2569

83014

01508 84852

You are old
now

tale resp?!

ness and the biological clock, who became lethally obsessed with a younger man. Again, if so much weren't at stake, I'd be tempted to laugh. Nothing could be further from the truth: he was, as you've probably deduced for yourself, obsessed with *me*. Those very tabloids that refer to me as "Humbertina" also describe me—with some accuracy, if I may say so—as "attractive," "sexy," and "stylish," not to mention "successful." So, I ask you, why shouldn't a younger man be interested in me, even obsessively so? *Have been.* Why, blind prejudice aside, should people find this so difficult to believe?

And as for his attorney's absurd allegations that I badgered him about his relationship with Patty, that I made abusive calls to her in Seoul, that I defaced photographs of her that I found in his apartment— well, what can I say? I've already established that, by this point, the end of May or beginning of June, I'd spent a total of perhaps thirty seconds in his apartment, certainly not enough time to decapitate every Polaroid in sight. And, to be perfectly honest, when he told me that he was going to tell Patty, so that he could, as he put it, "live in truth"—he'd been reading some inner-child self-help book, I suspect—my reaction was dismay. Patty was my insurance policy, my fire escape; I needed her as much as he did. More.

DEPOSITION OF PATRICIA LEE,
Interface Engineer, BrainWare International
445A Harrison Ave., Boston
January 25, 1995

OK, my name is Patricia Ann Lee, I'm twenty-eight, I'm a software engineer for BrainWare . . . is there anything else I need to say before I start? Oh, OK, I've known the . . . known Scottie since, well since 1988 I guess, though we really only started going together in our senior year, and then we moved to Boston together the next year, so that would have been '90, beginning of '90?

I don't really know what to say. I've never done anything like this before. It just feels extremely weird.

Excuse me? Oh, OK. OK, it was fine, most of the time—we got on well, had fun together, no major problems. Scottie could be really sweet, you know, when he wasn't in a bad mood or stressed out about work or something. Or stressed out about money, which was getting to be a bit of a problem by the time I left. For him, I mean, because he really wasn't making anything at *Things*—it was a joke how little they paid people over there. He wanted to find another job but couldn't decide what he wanted to do with his life, so he never

really, you know, looked for one? You know
what I think, I think his self-esteem just kind
of hit rock bottom when the band fell
apart.

Excuse me? Well, they didn't get any gigs,
except, you know, a few at the Middle East
and private parties and stuff like that, and
then the drummer left for another band, and I
think they all just looked at each other and
thought, why even bother.

Excuse me? Oh, the Mood Swings.

So then he got this job through his friend
Ted, taking pictures for *Things*, which he was
pretty good at actually, though he always said
how much he hated it. All he got to do was
the shopping section and the party page—
Robert, that was his boss, Robert kept all the
good assignments for himself, the interviews
and the club scene and so on, which I don't
think is fair, you know? And I think Scottie
was just kind of bummed out about what he
was doing: it wasn't what he'd had in mind
for himself, for his life, I think. Scott was—*is*, I
mean—a smart guy; he was a history major
when I met him, then switched over to film.
And then there was the band and . . . well,
one thing we did argue about in those days, I
guess, was the drugs—I don't do any kind of
drugs, period, and I could see that this stuff,
especially the coke, wasn't doing him any
good. It made him, I don't know, kind of
mean. No, not mean—more, like, impulsive,
irrational? Wouldn't take no for an answer.

Plus here he was saying how he didn't have any money and he was shoving it all up his nose.

Anyway, so it was a big problem for us when I got my promotion and had to decide whether to go to Seoul or not. I don't mean to brag but it was a pretty flattering offer, especially for someone my age, though naturally I know that being the token Asian had something to do with it too. At first he said it was cool, he was proud of me, but when I told them OK, I'd go in September, he started acting like a jerk, making sarcastic remarks about what a great time he'd have while I was gone and so on. But at the same time, sometimes when he was drunk or stoned, he'd break down, saying don't leave, don't leave. It was pathetic; I'd never seen him like that. I even thought about staying, but I said to him, I said, look, I care about you, Scottie, but I've got my own life to live too. It's only for a year. It's a good opportunity for both of us to focus on work, get our lives together—meaning him, really, I suppose, but me too.

We had all these plans for him to come visit, for us to do some traveling together while I was there, but of course he didn't have the money. I did pay for one trip, in December, so we could be together for the holidays, and we had a good time, I thought. Well, we did. He got to stop in Tokyo on the way back, which he'd always wanted to do—he really loves

Japanese movies, especially that one about the
noodle shop—so he was happy about that, I
know.

After that, I could tell something was up. He
was just weird on the phone, and sometimes
I'd call at two or three in the morning, his
time, and he wouldn't be there. The clubs close
at one A.M. in Boston, it's not like New York,
so I knew something was up.

Finally he told me that he was seeing this
older woman, but it was nothing, just sex. Sure
I was upset—like *really* upset: it seems so
selfish now—but what could I do? I was
twelve thousand miles away, I was working
like a dog, I just figured I'd hang in there and
hope it was a passing thing. Guys don't know
how to be alone, I know that. Everyone knows
that.

Then—well, then you know what happened.
His mother called me and I flew back to Boston.
I visit him every day now, in Mass. Eye and
Ear. The antidepressants seem to be helping
a lot.

We went back—for sentimental reasons, I suppose—to the Sechuan restaurant of our first
"date"—does it count as a date if you've already
had sex, I wonder, and are conducting the courtship
in reverse? Yet another problem of late-twentieth-
century nomenclature. *Boyfriend* is another. *Living
with.* And so on. Anyway, we went back to the

China Pearl, the good old gloomy China Pearl, where, squinting at our menus in the murk, I ordered moo shu, he, since the night was damp, a bowl of soup.

"Soup for two," the waiter said.

"No," he said, "just for one."

"Soup for two," the waiter insisted, pointing at the menu, where all the soups, indeed, were listed as "soup for two."

"Can't you make it just for one?" he asked, knowing I wouldn't want any because of the meat.

"Soup for two," the waiter replied.

"OK," he said, shrugging, "soup for two."

When it arrived, the soup was indeed soup for two, a small vat of it with a ladle and two bowls. We were at a table for four, so Scott put the second bowl on one of the unused place settings, to get it out of the way, I thought. But then he ladled both bowls half-full, took a sip from his bowl, moved into the vacant chair, took a sip from that one, moved back into his chair, took a couple of sips, moved into the other chair, sipped, and so on. As he did so, he assumed a different persona in each chair— avid and animated in the one, limp and lugubrious as soon as he moved into the next.

The waiter watched from across the room, stone-faced, his hands behind his back.

I laughed so much I choked on my moo shu.

Sometimes he was like that, fun to be around—playful and magnetic and vain, flashing kingfisher glances under his lashes like a movie star. But at other times, with unwashed hair and an old black sweater unraveling at the sleeve, he seemed to belong in a police lineup, his face drawn, his gaze inky and opaque. Then I'd notice, with distaste, the pitted scar on his left cheek, the tiny nerve that twitched intermittently under one eye. With Scott, you never knew who was going to show up; with Scott, it was always, somehow, soup-for-two.

Lexis/Nexis transcript, **Radio WTLK,** Boston, November 28, 1994

HOST: Today, folks, on SPEAK YOUR MIND, we have a very special guest, who perhaps can help us shed some light on the terrible tragedy that's rocked the Hub, the case that everyone's talking about, and about which we'll soon invite you to SPEAK YOUR MIND—I'm talking about the DeSalvo case, of course, which we've been following closely here since it broke last month. In a moment, we'll open up the phones and hear

from you, hear what *you* think about this
monstrous assault.

What do *you* think it tells us about violence in
American society? About the decline in family
values? Doesn't it make *you* wonder whether
feminism has gone too far? I'm wondering,
myself, whether white males are an endangered
species, in which case I'd better look out! We
want to hear what *you* think, but first I want to
introduce my guest today, Mr. Ted Rybczynski,
did I get that right, Ted?
GUEST: Ah, yeah.
HOST: Ted, tell our listeners how you know
Scott DeSalvo.
GUEST: Yeah, well, we used to play in a band
together and then the band broke up and I got
this job as music reviewer over at *Things*—the
magazine, well, it's more like a paper, really—
and then he came to work there too.
HOST: Great, Ted, and tell us: have you been
able to see your friend Scotty since the
accident?
GUEST: Yeah, I went over to Mass. Eye and Ear
last week but they only let me see him for five
minutes, about five minutes or so. He's got
bandages all over his face and stuff, you know,
really whacked out from the drugs. Never seen
so many flowers and cookies and stuffed animals
and shit in my life, either, from total strangers,
most of it, just cramming the place. Stacks of

mail, faxes, cards—like he can even read them, poor guy.

HOST: Poor guy indeed. And how were his spirits, Ted, on the day you saw him?

GUEST: Well, like I said, he was whacked out from the drugs. Totally.

HOST: Drugs?

GUEST: Yeah, to keep him from moving around too much, lifting his head, you know. He's not allowed to sit up or nothing, supposed to lay flat.

HOST: What an ordeal, what an ordeal for the poor young fellow. Did he say anything, Ted, about this Chandler woman, any clues as to what might have set her off?

GUEST: Nah. And I figure I'm not going to, like, bring it up if he doesn't want to talk about it. Give the guy a break.

HOST: Quite right, Ted. Any other insights for our listeners, anything else you'd like to add before we go to the phones?

GUEST: Yeah. I just wanna say that I'm sick of hearing people talk about Scott like he was just some kind of, you know, boy-toy. Scott's not dumb, OK? He was, I mean is, a really cool guy. Chicks liked him, he had this really cute girlfriend—it wasn't like he needed this crazy bitch in his life.

Way I see it, Scott had a lot going for him. Good-looking guy, smart, went to NYU, plus the guy's a really talented bass player. Or could

have been, anyway. He made these, like, really
cool videos when he was in film school. And the
guy *reads* all the time, man—well, used to—
books, newspapers, magazines, anything he can
get his hands on. When I went to the hospital, I
brought him Philip K. Dick and Günter Grass on
tape, because I know how much he loves those
dudes. So the guy's not dumb, OK?
HOST: OK, Ted, good point, we hear you. Now
let's go to the phones.

Against my better judgment, he went ahead and
told Patty—why, I'll never know. Naturally, I wasn't
privy to their discussions—nor, to be frank, do I
imagine that she had been leading a life of celibacy
in Seoul—but I do recall, vividly, the sounds that
he made after breaking it to her, the harsh, racked
sobs. It was the hardest thing he'd ever done, he
sobbed, he couldn't stop hearing how she'd wept, so
many thousands of miles away. He wept himself as
he told me, across my kitchen table, wiping his
nose with the heel of his palm.

"But," I asked him gently, "why? Why did you
have to tell her?"

"You know damn well why I had to tell her," he
said, his voice muffled through his hands. "You
know damn well."

I didn't—still don't. A mystery to me.

"But sometimes," I reasoned, "sometimes, surely, it's better *not* to tell everything. Sometimes leaving things out doesn't really count as lying at all."

"No," he said, raising his blotched face to look at me. "No, no, it's never better, how could it be?"

I shrugged. After my thirty-eight years, I wasn't so sure. "But what did she . . . ?"

"Oh God," he said, "what *could* she say?" And here again, a terrible dry howl.

Taking his hand, I led him to the bed, laid him down, and lay next to him, clutching his head against my heart with all my strength. He sobbed into the hollow of my neck, into the tender crevice above the clavicle, and as his tears touched my skin, a fierce joy surged through me, hemorrhaged through me, as if some membrane deep inside me had at last been torn.

MY LAWYER HAS asked me to note that the above represents a metaphorical use of language—no actual membranes or hemorrhages involved. Also, she has asked me to respond to the complainant's assertion that he remained on intimate terms with Ms.

Patricia Lee, that this same Ms. Lee continued to co-sign the lease on their shared domicile, 445A Harrison Avenue, that, in sum, he remained committed to his prior association with Ms. Lee throughout.

All I can say to this is, yes, he may on occasion have declared himself "committed to" Patty, but, as I asked myself at the time, what do those words mean, delivered in another's arms? And yes, her stuff did remain in his, I mean their, loft; her name remained on the mailbox and the answering machine, since she had no other U.S. address; they talked on the phone often, as old friends and old flames will do—but if she didn't realize that it was over, irrevocably over, then all I can say is that she chose not to. Chose not to confront the truth, which is, after all, how most people endure their lives.

WHILE WE'RE ON the subject, I just want to say that, when I mentioned Andreas earlier, I might have given a slightly misleading impression. I have no desire to see a distorted version of our affair smeared across the supermarket stands, followed by his equally distorted denials, so let me explain. He was, as I've stated, a fairly well known actor. *Is*. He was also, no doubt about it, an egomaniac, a liar, and what is so quaintly called a womanizer—but I knew that about him from the outset. I knew it from the second he switched on his bashful boyish smile and beamed it my way at the cast party after a benefit performance at the ART. I knew it and smiled right back. We spent that night together in his suite at the Charles Hotel, let him try denying that, but, since he lived in New York and was often off on location, I didn't see too much of him after that. In person, I mean. Ours was a grand passion sustained largely by the telephone and the fax machine, and, to a lesser extent, by the gargantuan beds of luxury hotels.

It did drag on for about two years: that much at least is true. And he promised to take me to Biba for my birthday, that's true too, though he never showed.

TV STAR DENIES "FURY" TIE
Boston Herald, December 8, 1994

Andreas Demos, dashing lead of the hot new TV series, "Soul Mates," denied yesterday that he had ever dated "Fury" suspect, Christine Chandler. Responding to a talk-show interview in which Demos' former Broadway co-star, "Red-Hot" Pepper Jenkins, claimed that Demos had dated

Chandler "on and off" for a couple of years, Demos told reporters: "I don't remember ever having met the woman in my life. And surely a woman like that, who could do such a terrible thing to a guy, would be pretty memorable!"

Appearing on Geraldo, Pepper Jenkins—a glamorous redhead whose name has also been linked romantically to the aquiline actor's— claimed that Demos dated Chandler "a few times, definitely" while both stars were in Boston for a season with the American Repertory Theatre. "I think it may even have dragged on after that," Jenkins stated. "She was one of those chicks that actors attract, you know, kind of a hanger-on type, not bad-looking, but a real loser."

Demos, interviewed on-set in Los Angeles, crinkled his brow in the lopsided, boyish fashion that has charmed millions of Americans since his TV character, Dude, made his debut last fall. "Look," he said, taking a sip of iced spring water, "I'm not going to say no, absolutely, I've never met this Christine Chandler, because I travel a lot, I meet a lot of women, if you know what I mean, and we're talking, what, at least a couple of years ago. But to the best of my recollection, I've never met her. The name doesn't ring a bell, the pictures I've seen in the papers don't ring a bell. And frankly, she's not my type!"

Demos, who reaffirmed his commitment to his fiancée and stunning "Soul Mates" co-star, Blair Belamour, conceded that he might, "just might," have met Chandler at a benefit dinner for ART in 1992, as Jenkins claims. "It's possible—" he said, "there were so many people there. And God knows, Pepper was watching me closely enough in those days! But anything beyond that, the idea that I ever really dated this Chandler lady, must be entirely in Pepper's head—or in the poor lady's head, which we all know is in sad shape." Asked if he would consider playing Scott DeSalvo in the upcoming TV movie based on Christine Chandler's life, Demos merely chuckled.

My lawyer is having difficulty finding anyone who can, or will, testify to having seen the complainant and myself together in public after the month of February or thereabouts. How *did* you spend your time together? she asks, as if for the first time entertaining a doubt. How do you think? I ask: We fucked. Fucked most of the night, until the wan city dawn began to drain the sky. Fucked till our bodies were raw and bruised. Fucked until one of us could take no more. Naturally we didn't always invite an audience, but, I tell her, there's a City of Boston road crew you could depose, a gardener at a country inn, a beachful of shell gatherers and dog walkers at the Cape. If you want witnesses, I can provide them.

Perhaps I should have provided them in the proper place, but I'm too tired and confused to go back now and figure out where, in this heap of scribbled yellow pages, the proper place would be. Chronology is much more taxing than it looks, a much more unnatural act.

I do know, though, that we went to the beach for a week in late June or early July—if I had my checkbook I could determine the exact date. At the beach house, an airy box of cedarwood and glass, we slept next to the French doors, waking at five to the brilliant surprise of the sun on the sea. We slept in the afternoons, too, when the light was tarnished and the air hardly moved. And we made love at all hours, knowing by then how to evoke, each time, a particular rapture, a particular cry.

Interesting how, even now, I find myself resorting to the language of the romance novel. It's either that, I suppose, or the language of torts.

On our last night at the house, we sat, wineglasses in hand, overlooking the sea. The sky was a lingering indigo, pierced by the first small stars. As the air grew chill, I got up to close the glass doors—without, I admit, replacing my clothes.

"Chris," he said, "don't move. You look great like that."

"Thanks," I said, striking a pose, "but I can't

stand here much longer because there are still people on the beach. And, if it's not my imagination,
they're looking this way."

"So what?" he asked.

"So nothing, I guess."

"So what?" he asked again, moving towards me.

"So what?" he repeated, snapping on a sudden
bright light. Like shop-window dummies, we stood
on display.

I tried to step around him but he blocked me,
shoved me back.

"So what?" he asked, cupping my buttocks
and ramming me hard against the cool panes of
the door. My flesh, I imagined, whitened and
spread, like the face of a child flattening its snout
on the rear window of a car, gargoyle of the motor-
way.

"So what?" he asked once more, freeing his
hands and pressing me against the glass until I
heard something crack. Then, facing the beach, he
knelt, and, like a dog, he licked me.

Depose the people on the beach, I tell her.

I'VE ALREADY TOLD you, I think, that early on—before everything went bad—the complainant and I

spent a weekend in the Berkshires. If I forgot to mention it before—well, consider it mentioned now, and let's move on to the morning after: the complainant and the defendant on the porch, in fluffy white bathrobes after their showers, drinking their coffee, slicing their scones, feeling lazy and limp and somewhat stunned from the night before. He looked, I recall, like a big clean baby, his skin a warm pink, his eyes milky blue.

I glanced up from my paper, saw him wholly absorbed in buttering his scone; saw, beyond him, the tender green grass; saw, above us, a sparkling sky. Life may have more to offer, I thought, but at this moment I can't think what it might be. Then, as if to chide me for that lapse, three loud coughing roars ripped through the quiet, followed by the unmistakable whine of an approaching lawn mower.

"Oh man," I said. "You'd think they'd do this on weekdays."

"Maybe it will move away," he said, but instead it came closer until I could see, quite clearly, the lean adolescent boy who was making his arc of effort over it, shirtless and, I noticed, apricot-skinned in the sun.

"Chris?" Scott said, after a while, and I realized

he'd been watching me, watching the kid. For, perhaps, some time.

"What?" I said, but he didn't reply. "What?" I repeated, my eyes wandering back.

"I'm here too," he said, clattering his cup onto its saucer. "You know?"

"I know," I said. "But what exactly is it that you're doing?" He had dropped, unexpectedly, to his knees. "Proposing?"

"No," he said, parting my robe near my feet.

"You'll get splinters in your knees," I said.

"No I won't," he said, peeling it all the way to my thighs.

"Scott," I said, "that kid can see."

"So?" he asked, peeling it further apart, tugging the sash so that it fell open, exposing me from the sternum down.

"No," I said. The kid was beginning to pay attention, beginning to turn the mower in deliberate swaths towards us.

"Yes," he said, burying his face in my lap.

"No," I said, "let's go inside."

His tongue was warm on my skin, on the inside of my thighs. The kid looped back and forth, closer each time, creating a high unbroken roaring rhythm. With his elbow Scott pried open my legs and then, with both thumbs, my sex. He found me with his mouth, blood-hot. I gasped, leaned back, closed my eyes, opened them, and then, till a spasm shut them, met the kid's unblinking gaze.

Depose the kid, I tell her.

SHE'S ALREADY DISCOVERED that there's no point in deposing my family and friends. Except for Angelica, they claim never to have met or even heard of Scott DeSalvo until both our names appeared spattered across the headlines. Well, I tell her, there are reasons for that. My parents live three thousand miles away, in San Francisco, and we communicate, as so many families do, by means of polite untruths. You could hardly expect me to discourse with them about my adventures involving a younger man and a pair of handcuffs. I'm an only child, too, which may or may not be relevant to my current plight—poor social skills, rich fantasy life, and so on, according to high-priced professional opinion. And yes, of course I have friends—Angelica, Julie, Steph (the sane one), even

Rosa, to name a few—but no particularly close ones, no. As far as I know, that's not a crime either.

Perhaps, I suggest, you might depose the dry cleaner, Stavropoulos, on Newbury Street. I left some clothes there for a while—weeks, maybe months—forgetting, in the accelerating disarray of my life, to pick them up. Ask Stavropoulos if he remembers one crumpled linen jacket, permeated with cigarette smoke; one pair of black leggings, rancid between the legs; one olive-green silk-blend sweater, ripped under the arm; and one satin camisole, stained with blood.

SOMETIMES HE STROKED my hair, soothingly, hypnotically, as if I were a child who couldn't sleep. Sometimes he touched his warm lips to my forehead, to my eyelids, to the back of my neck. Sometimes his flesh filled me, weighed me down, held me like gravity to the earth. At times like that, my body began to have some inkling of what it might be for.

Oh, I don't mean what you think I mean: I've read those books too, books about women like me, "career women," dupes of feminism who've sacrificed everything for money and power, only to wake up at forty alone, infertile, and afraid. I doubt that those books describe anyone, but they certainly don't describe me. I never had to give up anything, because, sadly enough, it doesn't seem to have been there in the first place.

Why not? I'm not sure. The only thing that occurs to me by way of explanation is something I once read about ants. In ant colonies, bear with me, the adult ants lick the larvae to keep them from growing moldy—not out of the goodness of their hearts, but because the larvae give off a sweet liquid that the ants enjoy. The adults also put food into the larvae's mouths because, when they do, they get a dose of that same sweet juice. Well, I must have been the larva that didn't give off the sweetness, that grew moldy from lack of licking—or am I, perhaps, confusing cause with effect?

For further details, subpoena my parents—if you can find them. They've changed their names, I'm told, since this all began.

EPSTEIN, CHANDLER, RICCIO,
AND BLACK
ATTORNEYS AT LAW
22 Market St., Suite 21
San Francisco, CA 94131

November 19, 1994

FOR IMMEDIATE RELEASE .... FOR
IMMEDIATE RELEASE ...... FOR IMMED

STATEMENT OF EVELYN AND
CARL CHANDLER

We, the parents of Christine Chandler, would like to reiterate our statement of November 2, 1994—namely, that we have no comment on the subject of the alleged assault on Scott DeSalvo and will continue to have no comment as long as the matter is *sub judice*. While we regret very much the injuries inflicted on Mr. DeSalvo, and wish him as complete a recovery as possible, we would like to emphasize that our daughter, Christine, is, as an adult, responsible for her own actions. We have no information concerning the alleged assault, and we appeal to members of the press to cease their harassment of us, our relatives, neighbors, and business associates. We have had no contact with our daughter since her arrest, nor do we intend to, though as parents we do feel obliged to offer financial support should she require it. We are as horrified as anyone else at the mutilation of Mr. DeSalvo, we pray for the restoration of his faculties, and we fervently request the media to respect our privacy in this time of great distress. Both Evelyn Chandler, Esq., and Carl Chandler, Esq., have taken indefinite leaves of absence from their respective employers, so we implore the media to refrain from disrupting normal business operations at these locations. Any further disruption will be met with prompt and appropriate legal action. The Chandlers have also temporarily vacated their Marin County home, so any future communications should be directed c/o Barry Epstein, Esq., at the above address.

In July, we went for a week to the beach—wait, I've already told you that. But did I mention that we went to the circus too, a one-ring, one-horse operation that toured the Cape? Inside the tent, the air was thick and yellow and popcorn-flavored, heady with the hum of children. We hunched like giants among them, clutching each other's hands till they were slippery with sweat. When the little boy next to me covered his ears during the clown routine, when he hid his face in his baseball cap, I secretly adopted him, offering him a peanut as tender of good faith. He was mine for the afternoon, he was ours, I pretended, our baby, our child.

"It's pathetic," I told Angelica afterwards, "*I'm* pathetic."

"It's just because there's no-one else around," she said with a shrug. "Lighten up and enjoy it while it lasts—it's harmless."

"Yeah," I said. "At least I know I'm doing this to myself. At least I won't go off the deep end."

"Oh, go off the deep end, it'd be good for you."

She leaned back in her chair and lit a cigarette, as if to ward off any more gauche confessions. They were beginning to bore me too, these pitiful little impulses of mine, so miserably misdirected. They also shamed me, alarmed me, thwarted all attempts at rationality, and filled me at times with such acute soaring sensation that I ignored the rest. The psyche finds ways to play five-finger exercises across the full emotional scale, I'd read somewhere, even in solitary confinement, even, presumably, in a cryogenic state like mine.

BACK NOW TO Boston in July, where we conducted our lives as usual except that, in search of air-conditioning, we went to the movies almost every night—old comedies at the Brattle, Fifties horror films, Jackie Chan, not really my cup of tea. And once in a while, as the talk shows have taken pains to point out, we watched pornography on the VCR. Doesn't everyone? If the media can get away with bribing video-store clerks for their customers' files, then nobody's private life is private any more—not even yours. Think about that for a moment before you leap to any conclusions based on a dubious title or two.

One night, at his loft . . . their loft. Whatever
you want to call it. Yes, I had begun spending more
time there—not much time, just the odd evening
now and then, until the incident I am about to describe. Any allegations to the contrary, allegations
that I kept showing up there and refusing to leave,
are simply laughable. If anything, I went out of my
way to avoid the place. My condo was altogether
cleaner and more comfortable, plus I thought it in
poor taste for him to have left a certain Polaroid
affixed to the refrigerator door. Its corners had
curled, its color had blanched, but her generous,
quizzical, caught-by-surprise smile had not.

Please note that I've never denied his attachment
to Patty. How could I deny it, since it was, literally,
staring me in the face? Obviously, we didn't discuss
their relationship in detail—in fact, he refused to
discuss it with me at all—but, piecing the story
together, I gathered that they'd both moved up to
Boston when she'd landed a job with a software
company. (A hot young company on Route 128: I
think you know the one I mean.) So of course he
must have been committed to her then—unless, as
a struggling musician, he'd merely followed the rent
check. They were, I presume, happy enough to-

gether and, given normal human inertia, would probably be together still if she hadn't moved to Seoul. Why, you may wonder, *did* she move to Seoul, if things were so peachy-creamy between them? A career move, apparently—a promotion, a one-year stint to set up a training program or something like that (I forget the details: perhaps someone can check her c.v. for me—Patricia Lee, NYU '89). He hadn't wanted her to go, he once told me, but, since she was out-earning him by a factor of five, he hadn't had much choice. So, what can I say? She took her chances like the rest of us.

Of course he was attached to her, but he was also young, and selfish, and a little spoiled. Restless, too. A middle-class boy from Connecticut, he'd never done anything irreversible, not even get a tattoo. He'd wanted to be a rock star, live dangerously, die young, but found himself instead, at twenty-six, photographing platform shoes for *Things*. Found himself wasted and bored, with no clue what to do next.

Of course he cared about her, but he was excited by me—by the sex, I imagine, by the license to act. By the intimations of what might yet come his way in life.

He was young, that's all. He hadn't yet learned that life won't let you have everything. Or, if it does, it certainly won't let you keep it.

WHERE WAS I? At his loft, their loft, whatever you want to call it, where, one night, we ended up in his bed. For the very first time, if you can believe that. We'd never yet had sex in his bed—in mine, yes; on his sofa, my sofa, the floor, the car, the beach, the porch of a country inn, and pressed against the rough wall of my entryway, but never in this bed: his bed; theirs. I admit, now, that it probably wasn't the best idea, especially in the face of his habitual demurrals, but that night he was drunk and hasty, and I, well, I suppose I was too.

Afterwards, he dozed face-down in his pillow as if poleaxed from behind; I lay staring at the ceiling, at the plaster crescent moon that curved around the blank where a light fixture had once been. Straining my eyes in the half-light that filtered through the blinds, I scanned the room like a radar beam, afraid of what I might miss, even more afraid of what I might see.

Piles of books and comics on an old dissecting table. A lava lamp. Tapes and CDs and CD ROMs.

Socks everywhere. A pair of fuzzy dice angled across a vacant picture frame. A news report enlarged to poster size: Kurt Cobain, Poet of Grunge Rock, Dead at 27. A huge jar of pennies, why didn't he cash them in? A mauve bathrobe, suspiciously small. Turning my back on that item, I yanked the bedclothes too hard and woke him up.

(Let me add, parenthetically, that I can't help blaming Patty for what happened next. If she'd had the grace, months earlier, to pack up and go—to remove her belongings from the premises, to unpeel her name from the buzzer on the way out—then this sordid little scene need never have occurred.)

"What?" he muttered, as he always did when startled awake, propping himself on his elbow as if to ward off blows.

"No, it's only me."

"Oh," he murmured, subsiding, then, looking around, realizing where he was, asked "What time is it?"

"Umm . . . one-fifteen," I said, peering at the green glow of the clock radio.

"Shit," he said, sitting up again. "I have to make a phone call."

"Now?" I asked.

"Different time zone," he muttered, climbing out

of bed and pulling on a pair of boxer shorts. He stumbled out, presumably to his desk.

I lay back, looked up again at the crescent moon, looked down again at the clock on the milk crate by the bed. Beside it lay three copies of *Rolling Stone*, an elastic knee brace, and a telephone. Damn you, I thought, and, heart beginning to speed, switched on the lamp.

I looked again at the bathrobe, draped over the corner of the closet door. I looked at the closet door, two or three inches ajar, and, in a fearful adrenaline flash, found myself out of the bed, across the room, snatching it wide open.

A jumble, a mess. A pair of crutches. Piles of dress shirts still in their cellophane. The sound of my own heart, spasmodic, like a frog. Shoes and videotapes and tennis rackets, and, on the floor, in the front, a small lilac something. A small twisted something. A small twisted pair of lilac underwear.

I untwisted it and peeled it apart where it was stuck, crusted together. I held it to my nose but smelt nothing: how long does that aroma last, I wondered, perhaps there's some scientific way of determining this. How long ago, doctor, did these juices, dried now like glue, flow wet from another woman?

Through the pounding in my skull, I thought I

heard a toilet flush, then a door open. Panicking, as if I'd been the one who'd committed a crime, I stuffed the underwear into the pocket of my jeans, which lay sprawled over a chair. Then, flushed and panting and tingling as if I had recently completed a marathon, I leapt back into bed and assumed the postcoital hands-behind-head position, marred only in this instance by my violent trembling.

"That was quick," I said.

"Couldn't get through," he replied. "All circuits are busy, blah blah blah."

"Oh," I said, "what a pity."

"Yeah," he said, abstractedly, taking a pocket calculator off the table on his side of the bed and fiddling with the battery compartment, saying "Shit" when the cover popped off and shot onto the floor.

"Come back to bed," I said, longing, absurdly, to be held.

"Mmm," he said, then, after a pause: "Chris?"

"Mmn-hmn?"

"Can I give you a ride home?"

"Now?"

"I'd be happy to."

"Are you crazy?" I said. "It's almost one-thirty, I just want to sleep." I was suddenly exhausted, as if all the adrenaline had drained out of my system, leaving me hollow and crumpled, a paper bag that someone had stepped on.

"I need to get up early tomorrow to do some work in the darkroom. Really early."

"OK, so we'll get up early," I replied, beginning, to my disgust, to whine.

He said nothing, bending to find the battery compartment cover and then trying, with surprising ineptitude, to force it back on. He gave up and put the calculator aside, in two pieces. I knew the tiny tongue of grooved black plastic would soon be lost.

"OK," he said, "I'll be honest."

"Do," I replied, with a sudden chill of fear. "That would make a nice change."

"I was trying to call Seoul."

"Surprise," I said.

"There's a twelve-hour time difference."

"I'm aware of that."

"If I don't get through to her, she'll probably call me. She's having some kind of crisis at work."

"Naturally," I said, with a mean, bitter edge to my voice, "she needs your support at a time like that."

"Yes," he said, brightening, as if pleased I'd understood. "And it wouldn't feel right to talk to her with you lying right here."

"No," I agreed, "that would be tacky. I'm glad your moral sensibilities are so refined."

He glanced at me, wary now.

"So," I added, "to save you any further trouble, I'll call myself a cab. Right now."

"You're not mad, are you?" he asked.

"No," I said, "I'm not mad." And I'm not fucking crazy either, you goddamn piece of shit, I thought: I'm calling a cab, I'm getting out of here, and I'm never going to see you again.

"Chris . . ." he wheedled.

White-hot with rage, I gathered my clothes from the various corners where they had been flung, and, shaking them out so that they made loud flapping noises, like sails, wriggled into my jeans, scratching myself with my own fingernails in my haste, showering small change onto the floor.

"Keep that," I snarled, reaching for the phone, "it's your tip."

"But Chris . . ." he repeated, his face beginning to flush a deep mauve-red, a shade I recognized.

"Shut up," I said, dangerously, and repeated his

address to the dispatcher. "Five minutes? OK. I'll be outside."

Outside, it had begun to rain, a hard, stripy rain like the rain that always falls in the movies. It battered me as I stood there, numb. But within the promised five minutes a cab did come into sight, crawling uncertainly down the street.

"Over here," I called, stepping into the road and waving.

He passed me, spotted me, zoomed back, and stopped. I climbed in, soaked. "Back Bay," I said. He cupped his ear, nodded, and released the brake so abruptly that the cab bucked before squealing off.

"So," I asked after a while, just to hear a human voice, "how's business? On a night like this?"

"Not bad," he shrugged and then glanced at me in the rearview mirror. "And yours?"

It took me a second or two before, with a surge of angry shame, I understood what he meant.

THE RECORD SHOWS, I hope, that by this point I had made at least two serious, good-faith attempts to sever my relations with the complainant—who, frankly, was becoming something of a drag. No, I didn't have time to go trawling for other men, so to an outsider my life might have appeared somewhat solitary, and certainly the complainant still exerted a powerful sexual pull on me, who could deny that. Most biologists now recognize the role of pheromones in human sexuality. But may I remind you that, as an intelligent, well-educated woman—Berkeley, Harvard Law, this is no time for false modesty—I am capable of recognizing a bad idea when I see one. And by this point my association with the complainant had become, clearly, a bad idea. From the start I'd sought to keep things light, casual, pleasurable; I'd relied on the existence of a third party to guarantee this effect; I most certainly had not contracted for absurd psychodrama involving third or fourth parties and their underwear.

Please. If I'd been looking for love, for marriage, for babies, as the prosecution has so spitefully suggested, would I have done so in the arms of an under-employed substance abuser twelve years my junior? Even my pheromones would have had more sense.

AFTER THREE DAYS—having called in sick, then unplugged the phone—I got out of bed and burrowed for my jeans in the laundry hamper. Burrowed through a pile of gamy tights and T-shirts, releasing my own stored aroma, musk and yeast.

I found the jeans, shook them out, and retrieved from one pocket the scrunched lilac twist. It looked much smaller and shabbier than I recalled.

Size 6, same as mine. Plain, with a prim lacy scallop around waist and thigh. An inexpensive department-store brand, according to the tag, where the trademark and other hieroglyphics—don't bleach, don't iron, don't wear during a lunar eclipse—had faded to a faint watery blue. 100% cotton, of course, exclusive of trim. The crotch was discolored and starting to sag.

Evidently not a woman who indulged in new lingerie for each night's rendezvous.

Patty, perhaps—a memento. Perhaps not. I wasn't sure which would be worse.

I crumpled it up and tossed it in the wastebasket, amongst the lipsticked tissues and razor blades. Then I immediately changed my mind, took it out, uncrumpled it, and pressed it smooth against my thigh. Not knowing what else to do, I pinned it to the corkboard in the kitchen.

No-one would see it there except me, and seeing

it would give me strength—the same kind of strength that allows a trapped animal to gnaw off its own limb.

Yes, it did occur to me that I might be losing my mind.

3

I'll admit that I felt a little depressed, a little down-in-the-mouth, over the next couple of weeks. Oh, nothing clinical—this is, after all, the age of Prozac—but rather a general sense of futility, a drizzle of malaise that even long hours at the office couldn't quell. Also, early August is a relatively slow time at work—the pace begins to pick up towards September, with the annual influx of F-1s and J-1s and H-1s—so, I suppose, time weighed more heavily than usual on my hands.

From my office window, I'd sit and watch people scurrying by in the neon-pierced dusk, their briefcases bulging, their heads abuzz with dreams and plans. As if any of it mattered, as if any of it would bear fruit.

"Firebomb Torches Tot," announced the headline on the tabloid in the bright yellow box as I waited to cross the street. Yes, well, I thought, as I headed home, that's the kind of world we live in.

Behind the elegant townhouses near the park, a man scavenged through the trash, shaking pizza boxes and take-out containers with agitated concentration. Something dark and furry snaked out of a bin, startling him, and was gone.

After that I kept my eyes down, staring at nothing but the few feet of sidewalk ahead of me. There was broken glass to negotiate, dog shit, grimy stepped-in wads of chewing gum, and flecks of foamy human mucus, spat up.

You needed a carapace to live here, and mine was cracked.

So EVERY EVENING I had a plan. I played squash three times a week, signed up for Advanced Spanish at Harvard Extension, and caught a movie with Stephanie most weekends, since Julie had started seeing someone in New York and was never around. He called himself a screenwriter—though others might have referred to him as a forty-four-year-old waiter—and had recently separated from a gay beau who, in parting, had broken his nose. As an afterthought, the beau had then committed mass murder by upending the fish tank onto the floor. Steph and I gave it two months, but we envied Julie the *Sturm und Drang*, not to mention the sex.

One evening, having nothing in particular to do, I opened a bottle of white Bordeaux and, standing in the chill humming light from the refrigerator's heart, drank it two-thirds down. Then, staring fixedly at a red dish towel, souvenir of Portugal, gift from my parents, noticing for the first time the rooster's mean beady eye, I emitted a sound that resembled a sob. Stop that, I instructed myself, right now.

Somewhat to my surprise, I obeyed my own instructions and found myself, wine bottle in hand, wandering around the apartment. Do something, girl. Anything. Put things away, there's an idea. Magazines into a neat pile on the coffee table. A tangled sweaty sports bra off the floor and into the laundry bag. Three days' worth of breakfast dishes washed up and dried. Dead petals picked off the tulips in their tall glass tube. Pennies organized into piles of ten.

Now what?

Two unread newspapers lay folded next to the fruit bowl; I was, I admit, mildly interested in the career of our local serial killer. The telephone bill, the gas bill, and the car payment awaited my attention. A button had come off my Agnès B. blouse, my pleated skirt needed ironing—again: why did I ever buy that thing?—and my nail polish was seriously chipped. The evening lay full before me.

But as I sat down on the sofa to read the *Times*, something opened inside me like a mouth, like a howl. I stared across the room at the empty grate, which stared back at me. Why hadn't I cleaned out those last fragments of charred brittle log? What if, after all these months, they by some mysterious thermodynamic process burst into flame? What if, while I slept, smoke curved back down the blocked flue, blackening my air; what if a spark should leap out, smoldering for hours in the rich pile of the Bokhara until it roared into violent life, consuming everything, the cherrywood tables, the velvety armchairs, the antique maps, none of it insured against conflagration because who, in the salesman's office, could have believed such extravagant destruction possible?

My lungs constricted and scintillae of light skittered across the Audubon print; I felt as if the salad I'd eaten for lunch was about to reappear in a viridescent stream. To keep it down, I swallowed another swig of wine, leapt up, turned on the television, turned it off (meaningless swirls and arrows across the planet's tired face, with some clown in a bow tie pointing here and there, "calling for" this and "calling for" that, as if any of it lay within his control). I went into the bathroom, washed off my makeup, and, staring at my own naked fissured mortal face, drank all the wine that remained. I then brushed my teeth, not neglecting to floss, took a Valium, and went to bed, where an uneasy unconsciousness sucked me down, into a dark maw of dreams.

LATE WINTER, BLEAK, but with some weak, gelid sunshine, almost enough to help me delude myself that the chill couldn't last much longer. So, after work, I'd walked home through the park instead of taking the train. It was almost warm enough to sit on a bench for a while, so, muffled and gloved, I did. The pond was no longer frozen; its surface, recently thawed, was desolate and slate grey, with thin slabs of ice showing how it had cracked.

A man in a camouflage jacket walked by and murmured something under his breath, which luckily I didn't hear. Then two little boys waddled towards me, strange creatures of about three or four, with wide, staring eyes, close-cropped orange hair, and a peculiar backwards-leaning gait. They might have been twins, out of Diane Arbus, though one was somewhat larger than the other. In their wake followed what looked like a mother and a grand-mother, both with that same slow weight-bearing waddle, like the one pregnant women adopt.

One of the little boys veered away from my bench and, eyes fixed on some distant point, somnambu-lated straight towards the pond. The grandmother, in complete silence, ran with a clumsy side-to-side roll to intercept him. Picked up, turned around, and pointed back where he came from, he continued like a wind-up toy back to the path, where he fell into step with his brother. They waddled on in syn-copation, both staring straight ahead, but this time the brother's hand, on some autonomous impulse, reached out and looped around the littler one's arm. For safety.

My eyes smarted. No, they stung, from the cold, the cold, the cold hopeless wind.

DEPOSITION OF ROSA GONZALEZ
Paralegal, Weisner, Bickey, & Taft
Boston
February 3, 1995

When I first started working for Chris in '93, spring of '93, I was, I don't know, intimidated? Such a smart woman, everything had to be just so, just perfect, you know, every little detail. Not just the paperwork and the appointment book, but everything—her clothes, her office, even the conference room, fresh flowers every Monday by nine A.M., otherwise you were in deep shit for the rest of the week. I was always afraid I'd mess up, forget something, make some little mistake, and be out the door, boom.

But actually it worked out well: I learned a lot, learned how to do things right, and if I did mess up once in a while, misplace a file or something, she'd never yell or curse, like Mr. Taft does sometimes when he's on deadline, she'd just make some kind of joke. Maybe a bit sarcastic, you know, but when you got to know her, you knew she was only joking, so you didn't feel too bad about it.

You probably won't believe me, after what's happened, but I thought she was a great boss, the best; she treated me well, always polite, apologized if she had to keep me late or whatever, gave me a real nice bonus at Christmastime. I even thought, if I ever get out of law school and pay off my loans, I'm going to dress like her, you know, real stylish—looks simple but you can tell it cost a bundle. Dark colors, usually. She kept a lint brush in her desk drawer and used it every time she left her office, I finally figured out.

Sorry. I'll try to get back on track here. Personal life? No. No way. We never talked about anything like that. I mean, I was her paralegal, not her girlfriend, you know, so *I* wasn't going to ask. Sometimes some guy would call the office and she'd say she didn't want to take the call, but I never asked who it was, didn't think it was any of my business, though, yeah, sure, I was curious. I figured she was beating guys off with a stick, anyway, nice-looking woman, nice body, nice clothes— why wouldn't she be? But no, I never actually saw her with a guy, no photos on her desk, nothing, not even family. I like to have a picture of my mom and my sister on my desk, my cat Bella, but I guess I don't see anything wrong with keeping your private life out of the office, either. Sylvia, one of the other paralegals, always used to joke around, call Chris "Closet Case" and all, but I just couldn't see that. I mean, *may*be—you never know, but . . . nah. I figured she was just real professional, you know. Well, she was. Totally. That's why this whole thing came as such a shock. Because I worked for her for a year and a half, almost, saw her just about every day, and I never even saw her get really mad, like Mr. Taft does. I mean, she'd get annoyed sometimes, a little short with people, the way everyone does sometimes at work, but I never saw her yell, never saw her lose it—except, OK, maybe once, towards the end, when some guy came to deliver flowers—for Amelia Bickey I think it was, from a client—and she just freaked out because he knocked on her door by mistake, I mean, *freaked out*. I figured it was PMS or something, because I'd never seen her like that.

Poor Chris. I just can't believe that this has happened to her. The guy must have done something to deserve it, that's all I can say. Jeez. Will you give her my regards when you see her? Is that allowed? Tell her everything's fine at the office.

As August wore on, I developed a new disorder, which no-one could explain. It began with odd pains, vermicular tinglings down my spine and deep into my chest, the rib cage too. Unable to sleep, I would follow each tiny impulse of pain through my body until it sputtered out and a new one sparked to take its place. My doctor gave me the usual perfunctory exam, the usual lecture about stress, and the usual pat on the back. The chiropractor, whom I was seeing twice a week for realignment, suggested that I come four times a week; she also suggested Rolfing, which terrified me—deep tissue damage—or acupuncture, which terrified me more. The herbalist, whom I was seeing for my allergies, suggested hot mud. Annoyed, I went back to the doctor and insisted that he refer me to a specialist.

"But a specialist in what?" he asked, with an amused air. It was time, once again, to find a new physician.

"A specialist," I explained, "in the kind of pain I'm experiencing."

"Well," he replied, "so far I've been unable to determine that it's of physiological origin."

"That's why," I said through gritted teeth, "I need a specialist."

I suppose that, while we're on the subject, I should provide a complete medical and psychological history, a no-holds-barred account of my asthmatic only-childhood in, well, let's just call it an affluent California suburb. Stories of how my underpopulated environment compelled me to play Single Parent Household instead of House, and so on. But, search as I might, no formative trauma springs to mind. The housekeeper never smacked me, as far as I can recall; the gardener never pulled down his pants. Good grades, good study habits, good manners, even; ballet classes, violin, horseback riding, and the poetry magazine. Not much time, in short, for acting out. In fact, the only confrontation I recall with either parent was the night that, at fourteen, I came home stinking of weed. Summoning me to her study the next day, my mother communicated her concern that I might damage my brain cells and never make it to Harvard Law, an argument that, I admit, gave me pause.

CHRISTINE D. CHANDLER
248 Commonwealth Avenue
Apartment 4C
Boston, Massachusetts 02116
(617) 555-1956

EDUCATION

Harvard Law School, Cambridge, MA
J.D. awarded June 1984, <u>magna cum laude</u>
<u>Executive Editor</u>, Harvard Women's Law Journal
<u>Associate</u>, Harvard Legal Aid Bureau

University of California, Berkeley, CA
B.A. in English/Psychology awarded
May 1979, <u>summa cum laude</u>
Elected Phi Beta Kappa (1978)
A. Davis Award for Academic Excellence (1979)
Charlotte Kinbote Prize for English Essay (1979)
Banville Prize for Rhetoric (1979)

EMPLOYMENT

Weisner, Bickey, & Taft, Boston, MA
<u>Partner</u> (1993 to present)

<u>Immigration/Asylum Associate</u>
(Sept. 1986–1992)

<u>Summer Associate</u> (Summer 1982, 1983)

Refugee Rights Project, Cambridge, MA
<u>Project Coordinator</u> (1989 to present)

Northeastern Law School, Boston, MA
Faculty Member (1988–89 Academic Year)
Taught appellate advocacy, legal writing and
research

Professor Marcia Albright, Cambridge, MA
Research Assistant (June 1983 to June 1984)

In this context, I should, I suppose, mention one
more thing: that my parents, being lawyers, didn't
always tell the truth. To me or, as I later discovered,
to each other. This caused some confusion while
I was growing up, certainly, but it now strikes me
as a ubiquitous, even axiomatic feature of family
life. Yet another reason to avoid it. Another reason
not to reproduce—oneself, I mean, and, thereby,
it.

CHANDLER HOUSEHOLD A
"HOUSEHOLD FROM HELL"
EXCLUSIVE!
Former Housekeeper Breaks 30-Year
Silence

*"IF ABORTION HAD BEEN LEGAL, YOU'D
NEVER HAVE BEEN BORN!" CAREER-
MOM TELLS CHRIS*

*DAD'S SAUCY SAUSALITO HOUSEBOAT!
EXCLUSIVE PICS, P.3*

The National Investigator, December 9, 1994

"Boston Fury" Christine Chandler grew up in a "household from hell," characterized by scream-ing fights and sleazy affairs, according to her fam-ily's former housekeeper, Luz Alvarez. "I've been quiet for thirty years," said Alvarez, speaking from her village in the remote Chiapas highlands, where an *Investigator* reporter had tracked her down, "but now it's time for me to speak. Poor girl, this Christina, I remember her well."

Alvarez, now a sprightly 74, went on to describe a family life that, while picture-perfect from the outside, involved hideous bouts of (continued on p. 3)

STATEMENT FROM THE OFFICE OF
LIONEL MORRIS, M.D.
Berkeley, California
December 12, 1994

To protect his clients' right to privacy, Dr. Morris will neither confirm nor deny having treated specific indi-viduals in the course of his clinical practice. Dr. Mor-ris is therefore unable to confirm or deny published reports that he treated a Ms. Christine Chandler for depression in 1971, 1976, 1980, or at any other time. Nor is Dr. Morris able to comment on any referrals that he may or may not have made to fellow mental health professionals. Dr. Morris, who is available for inter-views on other topics—including his recent findings on fluoxetine and dysthymic personality disorder—respectfully requests the media to honor the confidentiality of the psychotherapeutic relation.

Allow me to point out, at this juncture, that if the complainant had indeed been desperate to disembarrass himself of me, then the last two weeks of August would have been the time for him to do just that. All he would have had to do, in fact, was nothing: I refused to see him, to take his calls, to read the goofy little postcards he sent, signed not with his name but with his doodle, a scribbled stick figure with an oversized camera for a head. (Let others probe the psychoanalytic implications of this.) I'd seen Mr. Camera-Head before and knew that he could look, as the occasion demanded, happy, sad, rueful, or coy. This time, I noted—en route to the recycling bin—that old Camera-Face was looking distinctly out of sorts. Borderline psychotic, one might even say.

Admittedly, that might be overstating the case: the plaintiff wasn't that gifted an artist, and it was, after all, just a childish cartoon, designed to endear. And there was, I suppose, something endearing about it—about the transparency of its intentions, its eagerness to please. . . . Anyway. My point is that if Mr. DeSalvo had so wished, he could easily have

vanished from my life during those two weeks—
vanished, evaporated, the way a perfume will do—
your Opium, your Obsession—if you neglect to stop
the vial, leaving only the lingering revelation of its
cheapest ingredients.

But did he? No. Instead, he—well, *harassed* is
probably too strong a term but he, shall we say, made
frequent and energetic attempts to communicate
with me. At first, as I recall, he took a wheedling
tone—*Hey, Chris, sorry about last night, I know it
wasn't cool, but you know, sometimes stuff like that's
going to happen; I'm sorry, there's not a whole hell of
a lot I can do about it, don't be mad, give a call back
and let's hang out tonight*—that kind of approach.
Then, as one might predict, his messages became
more defensive, more along the lines of *Hey, Chris,
what is UP with you? I can't believe you're acting like
this over one little phone call. At least talk to me—
this is so dumb, Chris. Chris? Come on, let's at least
talk. I don't understand why you're so mad all of a
sudden. I mean, it's not as if you didn't know that I
spoke to Patty on the phone sometimes. So, big deal. I
don't understand why it's suddenly such a big fucking
deal. Chris? Chris? I know you're there.* And then
these late-night laments began to degenerate into
random ramblings, into long broken jeremiads about

his loneliness, his shitty job, his bad haircut, his asshole dad, his craving for sex. Sometimes, pausing for breath or to find the next word—or to take what sounded like a large gulp of a large drink—he would pause too long and the machine, with ruthless promptitude, would cut him off.

I saved all these tapes—or, at least, I'm almost sure I did. Maybe Laurie can find them for me: they're probably neatly stowed in a box labeled TAPES. He said, I think, "I miss you." He must have said "I need you." He said "You're the only one I can talk to."

NYNET	Account number	**617 555-1968**
	Billing Date	**Sept 1, 1994**
	NYNET	Page 1

Service to   R. Scott DeSalvo
              445A Harrison Avenue
              Boston, MA 02118

. . . .

NYNET
Summary of account

Previous charges and credits

Amount of last bill	$483.29
Payments through Aug 30. Thank you	00.00 CR
Amount past due	**$483.29**

**PLEASE NOTE THAT YOUR ACCOUNT IS SERIOUSLY OVERDUE.
FAILURE TO PAY PAST-DUE AMOUNT MAY RESULT IN
SUSPENSION OF TELEPHONE SERVICE**

Current charges

NYNET	$00.25
MTI Telecommunications	384.80
Total current charges	$385.05

Total amount due	$868.34

Payment is due on September 21, 1994

<u>Itemized calls</u>

<u>Directly dialed</u>

No.	Date	Place called	Number called	Time	Rate	Min.	Amount
1.	July 23	Boston MA	617 555-1956	2:36 am	Night	1	.07
2.	July 31	Boston MA	617 555-1956	11:42 pm	Eve	1	.07
3.	Aug 07	Boston MA	617 555-1956	3:17 am	Night	2	.11
						Total	$ .25

MTI

International Long Distance

Calls from 617-555-1968

No.	Date	Time	Place	Area-Number	Min.	Amount
1.	July 22	1:22 am	SEOUL SK	01822	1	1.30
2.	July 22	1:36 am	SEOUL SK	01822	1	1.30
3.	July 22	2:09 am	SEOUL SK	01822	47	61.10
4.	July 24	12:16 am	SEOUL SK	01822	28	36.40
5.	July 27	12:02 am	SEOUL SK	01822	52	67.60
6.	July 31	11:39 pm	SEOUL SK	01822	1	1.30

7.	Aug 01	1:11 am	SEOUL SK	01822	74	96.20
8.	Aug 04	2:47 am	SEOUL SK	01822	89	115.70
9.	Aug 07	3:15 am	SEOUL SK	01822	1	1.30
10.	Aug 08	4:20 am	SEOUL SK	01822	1	1.30
11.	Aug 09	12:01 am	SEOUL SK	01822	1	1.30

Total International Long Distance   **$384.80**

Thank you for using MTI

*You saved $19.22 on calls to your **Friends Around the World!***

I tried, believe me, not to think about him, I tried all the time, but my life had become a mine field of involuntary flashbacks, triggered by the most quotidian acts. Taking a shower, for instance, or walking down my front steps.

Once, drenched in sweat after sex, I'd left him sleeping and gone to bathe. The sound of the shower had woken him, so he'd climbed out of bed, carried a kitchen chair into the hallway, sat there, and—through the open bathroom door, through the clear plastic shower curtain with its fine white stripes, through the beads of moisture massing there—he'd watched. Like a paying customer, he watched. Until I stepped out and, dripping, straddled him.

Once, sitting on my front steps, I'd watched him park his car—watched, in a starburst of joy, the complainant parking his car. He hadn't seen me yet—I was out there in the dark, trying to catch what little breeze there was—and I watched, watched his tense, distracted face kindle into radiant cockiness as a Jeep peeled out from a parking space ahead. Zipping forward and backing in, he twirled the steering wheel in a showy, one-handed way that filled me—don't ask me why—with intolerable tenderness. To anyone else, he would have looked like a twenty-six-year-old guy parking a car. To me, though—and this is something I can't explain, something fearful but true—he seemed to represent the end of an ice age, the beginning of the possibility of life on earth.

Perhaps that's why I gave in once again, gave in to his pleas and his pressure tactics. Life doesn't always make sense when you try to explain it, does it, which is why most people end up telling lies. Not that I am—though bear in mind that the truth doesn't always sound true, either.

Prisoners in solitary confinement, I've read, sometimes induce pain as an antidote to the unendurable absence of sensation. They scarify their flesh, for instance, sear themselves, starve. I offer this as an analogy, nothing more.

* * *

ANYWAY, THIS IS how it happened, as best I can
recall. Arriving home from work one evening,
around nine or so, I trudged up the three flights of
stairs, and, as usual, unlocked the door, dropped
the mail on the hall table, pushed each shoe off
with the other foot, put my briefcase on the chair,
unbuttoned my suit jacket, and hung it up. (The
sequence never varied: after the mail came the
shoes, after the shoes came the bag, after the bag
came the coat, after the coat, I suppose, came old
age, sickness, and death.) This time I added the
most recent twist—a shot of Stoli from the freezer—
then headed to the living room to check my messages.

The living-room door had blown shut, and when I
nudged it open, taking care not to spill my drink, I
gasped. Where I'd left a spare, orderly space, I'd
returned to a shambles, a crash site of broken stems
and battered blooms, with an insistent dripping
sound from a tall glass vase lying on its side and
funneling its remaining water, drop by drop, onto
the floor. The curtain, still bellying vigorously in
the breeze, had knocked over an enormous vase of

stargazer lilies—which had not been there that morning when I left.

I felt a sudden strong urge to sit down, so I did, right there on the rug, where, chin on knee, I contemplated a lily's snapped head, breathed its rich, bruised scent. I watched the slow seep of water across the wooden floor. I wondered, once more, if I might be losing my mind. Then, glancing around, I saw the note.

He had been in my apartment.

He had left the flowers and the note. Scrawled on the back of a postcard—Magritte, I believe—his message had somehow landed in the fireplace, though I deduced, from its probable trajectory, that it had been propped against the vase. "Chris," it said, "I miss you." (No of course I cannot produce it now: I must have thrown it out.)

His number was still programmed into my phone, so it took only one violent jab to reach him, which was just as well, since my hands were shaking. With anger, I suppose, but also, perhaps, with another kind of incredulous agitation— with a sensation similar to what I imagine a kite might feel when, finally catching the current, it rises, curved and tense with air, aloft at last.

"How the *hell*," I asked, in a strangled voice, "did you get into my apartment?"

"Easy," he replied, and I could picture him shrugging, doing the sheepish smile. "The building manager let me in."

"The building *manager* let you in?"

"She recognized me—she's seen me before, coming to visit you, I guess. I had an armful of flowers, so I must've looked harmless, and I convinced her that they were a birthday surprise for you, that I wanted you to find them there when you got home."

"The building *manager* let you in? Goddammit, she'll barely let *me* in when I've lost my keys."

"She was really nice. She even gave me a glass of iced tea."

"She invited you into *her* apartment, too?"

"Yup. In her housecoat, some kind of housecoat thing."

"I wouldn't get too excited about that," I retorted. "That's all she ever wears." That was also, unfortunately, how I knew his story was true.

I am well aware that the woman in question, Mrs. Jean Malloy, has denied everything—denied giving him access, denied the iced tea. Well, she'd have to, wouldn't she, if she wanted to keep her job.

Plus, as my neighbors will attest, the poor creature is a notorious drunk, given to strange fits of amnesia and facial agnosia—she once chased me up the stairs, demanding to know who I was, after I'd lived there for five years.

Of course, it is also possible that she's telling the truth, that she *didn't* let him in, and that he'd already made a copy of my key. In fact, the more I think about it, the more plausible that seems.

DEPOSITION OF MRS. JEAN MALLOY
Building Manager, 248 Commonwealth Avenue
Boston
February 10, 1995

Note: The deposition of Mrs. Jean Malloy has had to be postponed indefinitely, because the witness is currently confined to Massachusetts General Hospital, awaiting a liver transplant.

Yes, I did allow him to come over later that night. After he begged. For quite some time.

Well, what would you have done? I was beginning to feel a little uneasy about the way the situation was developing, a little jittery perhaps. Wouldn't you have? And wouldn't you have allowed him to come over, to discuss matters calmly, face to face, instead of cowering at home with a chair-back wedged under the doorknob, wondering what he'd do next? He'd already broken—or conned—his way into my apartment once that day, remember.

So, yes, he came over; he rang the buzzer, and I opened the door. (If that's a crime, I plead *nolo contendere*—*nolo contendere* to everything, in fact.) He kept his hands in his pockets and refused to meet my eye; his Talking Heads T-shirt had seen better days. A musk of damp sweat arose from him, as it probably did from me—Boston by the end of August is a bouillon of heat and stress and petrochemicals, the air thick and adversarial, accosting you like a mugger as soon as you step outside.

I didn't say anything. Neither did he. His mouth was set in a straggly *M*, a child's effortful pout. He looked at me. He looked down at his Docs. He looked at me again. Then, in a sudden wordless move, he slipped his hands out of his pockets and pulled me towards him, pressing me against the bones of his chest until I emitted, like a squeaky toy, a sound.

Love, I thought, as I clasped him back—an abstract noun; a term of endearment; a score of zero.

BATTERED WOMAN SYNDROME
SEEN AS MOST LIKELY DEFENSE
New York Times, January 31, 1995

Legal experts and forensic psychiatrists are far from unanimous in their evaluation of the Christine Chandler case, recent interviews revealed, and offer widely differing predictions, ranging from battered woman syndrome to Prozac abuse, of her probable defense. Ms. Chandler, the 39-year-old Boston attorney who maimed her young lover, Scott DeSalvo, 25, in a gruesome attack last October, faces trial on charges of mayhem, assault, and attempted murder. Though preliminary hearings are expected to begin in June, Laurie Katz, the high-priced feminist lawyer who is leading Ms. Chandler's defense team, has so far given no indication of what strategy the defense intends to pursue. "There'll be time enough for people to discover the whole, horrible truth once trial begins," said Ms. Katz, who declined further comment.

However, interviews with legal and psychiatric experts reveal a range of possible defense strategies, with little consensus on what Ms. Katz will plead. "So much is going to depend on the composition of the jury," said Marcia Albright, author of "Women on Trial," "that it's useless to predict anything until we see what Laurie manages to get."

Other experts were, however, more willing to venture an opinion. "Understand, here, that I'm speaking extremely hypothetically," said Bryan

Berkowitz, the Stanford professor and celebrity defender, "but, in a similar situation, based on what I've read so far, I'd have no hesitation going with battered woman syndrome. You've got the abusive sexual set-up, you've got the exposure to violent pornography, you've got what looks like a legitimate fear of *Continued on Page C5, Column 2*

The next morning, he walked me to the subway stop, where he kissed me good-bye—once on the lips, once more on the cheek. Then he turned around and, thumbs hooked into belt, shambled off with his peculiar, rapid, forward-listing gait, a gait that always reminded me that walking is, in fact, just a repeated act of recovery from falling down. Sometimes it struck me as endearing, this walk of his, at other times absurd. That day it sent a hot violent stab through me.

In the evening, I took that thing—that lilac thing—off the bulletin board and threw it in the kitchen trash, amongst the apple cores and coffee grounds. He hadn't noticed it yet, and, given the quality of attention he usually invested in his surroundings, he probably never would. But a small knife-twist of shame turned in my gut every time I thought of it; the whole episode now struck me as sordid, perverse. Whatever he might have done, I'd sunk equally low: illegal search and seizure, theft, knicker-sniffing to boot.

Taking the bag from the bin, I knotted its black neck and dumped it in the alley like a corpse. I would, I decided, never mention that unmentionable, never allude to that little spasm of madness.

Of course, as the record shows, I eventually did—it's the kind of thing that tends to pop out under stress, isn't it, a jack-in-the-box in the brain. The mind is a mooncalf, unable to follow the most explicit instructions (don't think about that, don't bring that up). The mind is a half-wit, unfit for its job.

4

THE VERY PRIVATE LIFE OF CHRISTINE CHANDLER:
FRIENDS, CO-WORKERS BAFFLED BY TRAGIC ACT
Boston Globe, December 11, 1994

This much, at least, is beyond dispute: Monday, Oct. 31, 1994, was a crisp and cool autumn day in Boston, hinting by nightfall at the cruel winter to come. For Christine Diane Chandler, a 38-year-old Harvard-educated attorney, it was a normal working day. She took the Green Line downtown to her office at 7:30 a.m., returned to Back Bay around 8:45 p.m., ate a hasty meal of Thai take-out, drank a couple of beers, and retired early. But something else happened that night, too. Shortly before midnight, in the spotless kitchen of her Commonwealth Avenue condominium, Chandler assaulted her 25-year-old lover, Reginald Scott DeSalvo. The bloody attack left DeSalvo, a staff photographer for *Things* magazine, maimed and blinded in both eyes.

This much both Chandler and DeSalvo agree on. But everything else about that fateful night, including Chandler's motives and the chain of events that led up to the assault, remains clouded in doubt. Though the case has seized the national imagination, prompting hours of talk-radio debate, little, if any, light has been shed on what happened between the two lovers behind those closed doors.

Chandler, who was released on bail last month, remains in McLean Hospital under psychiatric surveillance: she faces charges of mayhem, assault, and attempted murder, with preliminary hearings expected to begin by May of next year. In her sole statement to date, an apparent confession made shortly after her arrest, Chandler does not deny responsibility for the attack, nor does she substantially dispute DeSalvo's account of that evening's events. However, Chandler's attorney, Laurie Katz, has claimed that her client acted in response to a perceived threat on her life.

DeSalvo, on the other hand, has issued a written statement denying that he ever threatened or abused Chandler, with whom he had been romantically involved since early January. Declining, on medical grounds, to grant any interviews, he claims that his former mistress, distraught over his attempts to end the relationship, assaulted him unprovoked.

The facts of the matter will be decided in a court of law, but, in the meanwhile, friends and relatives of both parties are still reeling with shock and disbelief, trying to make sense of an apparently senseless act. "The question," says Dr. Phyllecia Lofton-Browne, an expert on domestic violence, "is not so much what happened that night as why. And that is something we may never know."

What is known is that at 11:56 p.m. that cool October evening, Chandler dialled 911, calling for emergency assistance at her Commonwealth Avenue address. In flat, unemotional tones—familiar now to radio listeners from a much-aired police tape—she instructed the dispatcher to send an ambulance, stating that there had been "an accident, a bad accident." But when police and paramedics reached the fourth floor of the Back Bay brownstone, they found a gory spectacle befitting Greek tragedy: the handsome young DeSalvo lay semi-conscious on the kitchen floor, bleeding profusely from severe injuries to both eyes.

"Mr. DeSalvo had undergone what we call complete bilateral ocular enucleation," explained Dr. Vivek Ramsani, chief of ophthalmology at Brigham and Women's Hospital, where DeSalvo was treated for trauma. "To put it in layperson's terms, both eyeballs had been torn from their sockets. This is something that, under extreme circumstances, a person could do with her bare hands, with her fingernails—as apparently occurred in this case."

DeSalvo (who goes by his middle name, Scott) remains hospitalized at the Massachusetts Eye and Ear Infirmary, where he is undergoing intensive rehabilitation, physical therapy, and treatment for depression. Doctors say that the budding young photographer, now 26, will never regain his sight. "There are no words to describe the tragedy of this young life struck down, ruined, deprived of his art," said Dr. Erica Collins of Mass. Eye and Ear, "but our job is to prepare Mr. DeSalvo to live a useful and even joyous life when he leaves here. Millions of partially sighted and differently abled individuals do just that."

While DeSalvo tries to put his shattered life back together, Chandler's friends and co-workers, still stunned by her arrest, are asking themselves how the Christine Chandler they knew—a stylish, successful Harvard graduate, a tireless volunteer for Boston's Haitian community, a woman who rarely displayed any emotion—could be implicated in such a heinous deed.

"There must be some mistake, that's all I can tell you" said Rosa Gonzalez, 28, Chandler's assistant at the law firm of Weisner, Bickey, & Taft. "The Chris I knew would never have been capable of doing such a thing. She just wouldn't have. That's all I have to say."

Chandler's colleagues at Weisner, Bickey, & Taft have refused all comment, beyond a short statement released on the day after Chandler's arrest. "We at Weisner, Bickey, & Taft wish to express our shock and outrage at the crime of which our colleague and partner, Christine D. Chandler, stands accused," the statement reads. "We shall have no further comment on the matter while it remains *sub judice.* We know Ms. Chandler only as a brilliant, dedicated, and highly qualified colleague, revered amongst Boston's Haitian community for her work with the Refugee Rights Project. Never has Ms. Chandler displayed any but the strictest professional demeanor in the workplace or with clients, and we trust that her current misfortunes will in no way reflect on the good name of Weisner, Bickey, & Taft."

While Chandler's academic and professional qualifications are unimpeachable—a summa cum laude graduate of the University of California at Berkeley, she graduated from Harvard Law School near the top of her class—her personal life remains a matter of some conjecture. Is it possible, as some published reports have suggested, that this seemingly career-oriented young woman lived a shadowy double life?

Interviews with Chandler's acquaintances paint a portrait of a somewhat solitary, driven individual, committed above all to her work. Chandler's workaholic lifestyle left little time for relaxation or a personal life, let alone for romance, according to Juliet Duverger, Associate Professor of French at Boston University. "In fact," said Duverger, "I didn't even know she had a boyfriend until this whole thing hit the, the papers." Duverger, who described herself as Chandler's "closest friend, her confidante," said that Chandler was "a very, very private person." But, Duverger added, "she knew she could open up to me. And she never did, not once, all the time this situation was brewing. And that's what I find so amazing about the whole thing."

Chandler's parents, Evelyn and Carl Chandler of Marin County, California, have refused to speak to the media since their daughter's arrest, so information about Chandler's early years remains scant. What is known, however, suggests a privileged and apparently untroubled childhood as the only child of affluent parents, both of whom still practice corporate law in San Francisco.

Although certain revelations about the Chandler household have recently surfaced, these allegations, derived mainly from a housekeeper who was dismissed in 1965, have yet to be independently confirmed. "You have a tainted source, a disgruntled former employee," said Dr. Peter S. Liebling, dean of Boston University's College of Communications. "You have memories that are 30 years old, suddenly put up for sale. In other words, you have checkbook journalism. So I would take it all with a big grain of salt."

The known facts are these: born on July 13, 1956—three days before her mother, Evelyn, took and passed the California Bar exam—Christine Chandler attended Berkeley's famed Montessori School, graduating in 1967 to the exclusive Wheatley Girls' Academy in Walnut Creek. Teachers there recall her as a bright, diligent student, an accomplished violinist, and editor of the literary magazine.

"You never had to tell Christine anything twice," said Vera Mackay, Chandler's 11th-grade Latin teacher. "She was very responsible, very anxious to please, a hard worker. A straight-A student, of course. None of the usual adolescent attention-seeking, you know, no smoking or miniskirts, none of that nonsense."

At the University of California at Berkeley, where Chandler double-majored in English and psychology, she maintained a 4.0 GPA—at the cost, apparently, of a normal undergraduate social life. "Chris didn't really like to get down, hang out with the rest of us, drink beer and all that other stuff we were doing at Berkeley in the Seventies," said Amy Isserman, now chief film critic for the Los Angeles Times. "She probably has more brain cells to show for it now than we do, though! She and I took a whole bunch of English classes together, but I don't really remember any close friends, any serious boyfriends—sure, she would date guys, have sex with them, I assume, since we all did in those days, before the plague, but she always said she didn't have time for anything more. She just studied so hard, plus she was always involved in some kind of political work— women's issues, the prison project, I forget what all else. But hanging out? Forget it."

At Harvard Law School, where Chandler held a high-profile position as executive editor of the Women's Law Journal, she was renowned, even among law students, for her workaholic ways and for the long hours she put in at the Legal Aid Bureau.

"Look," said one of her former professors, who requested anonymity, "Christine is an unusual person, an admirable person in many ways. She could have done anything she wanted, could have gone the corporate route, but instead she chose immigration law, which is not, how shall I put this, the most prestigious branch of the law. In fact, to put it bluntly, it's mostly grunt work and it pays horribly. But that's what Christine wanted to do.

She'd already had some experience working with refugees, in Berkeley I think, and she just made up her mind that this was the kind of work she wanted to do. With all her skills, all her advantages, that's what she chose to do. Even though I thought she was nuts at the time—and I guess I still do—you sort of had to respect her, respect her stubbornness, if nothing else. Stubborn as a *mule."*

During her years at Harvard Law, Chandler shared a Cambridge apartment with a fellow graduate student, now a Boston-area professional, who declined to speak for attribution. "I don't know how you tracked me down," the former roommate said, "but I really have nothing to tell you." Asked if he and Chandler were on intimate terms, the ex-roommate replied: "I'm sorry, but I don't see that that's anyone's business, 15 years down the line."

How the path of Christine Chandler finally crossed that of Scott DeSalvo, an NYU graduate and would-be punk guitarist, remains something of a mystery. "She must have picked, I mean, met him at a bar," said Duverger, the French professor. "There's this bar, Twenty-Nine, where a friend of hers worked, and sometimes she'd stop there on her way home from work." But Ted Rybczynski, DeSalvo's close friend and former bandmate, claimed that DeSalvo met Chandler while covering an event at the Institute of Contemporary Art for *Things.* "I personally never met this girl," Rybczynski said in a recent radio interview, "but I remember Scott telling me about some chick he picked up at the ICA, so that must of been her."

In yet another version, *Boston* magazine has reported that the two met while playing squash at the exclusive Tennis and Racquet Club; the Back Bay institution, as a matter of policy, declines to release any information regarding its membership.

However the couple may have met, their romance blossomed during the spring and summer of 1994 until—according to the manager of Chandler's brownstone, who lives on the premises—DeSalvo was visiting Chandler almost every night. Oddly enough, the lovers never introduced each other to friends or family, preferring, it seems, to spend their time quietly at home together. Quietly, that is, until the night of Oct. 31, when the silence that surrounded their affair was broken forever.

"We may never understand the needs that draw two people together, or keep them together," asserted Lofton-Browne, the authority on domestic violence. "What we do know, though, is that when an interpersonal situation explodes into violence, you can be sure it didn't happen overnight, that in some ways, it's taken the two individuals their entire lives to reach that point." And in the life of Christine Chandler—straight-A student, star of Harvard Law, champion of the dispossessed—there seems to have been much more than met the eye.

You may be wondering by now why I resumed my relations with the complainant—took him back, went back to him, whatever you want to call it. I've been wondering much the same thing myself. To save time, I suppose we could agree that it was simply a matter of sex and move on—as if sex were ever that simple.

We did not, at that point (early September, record-breaking heat) discuss the recent rupture in our relations. For a while he was tender and solicitous, bringing me flowers and blackberry tea, as if I were convalescent, which, in a way, I was. He even brought his tool kit over one night, to help me put up some shelves. And we spent more time together, too, listening to music, eating out, watching the news . . . no, I'm not stalling, not straying from the point, as my lawyer has so ungenerously suggested: I want to tell you everything, the good, the bad, and the trivial, otherwise how will you ever understand?

We also fucked a lot, or rather, I fucked him, frenzied, lustful, full of heat.

Sometimes, when I slammed the door behind us, shoved him against it, and writhed into him, clawing his hair, I couldn't tell whether it was lust or rage that drove me. Sometimes, when I clutched him so hard that we overbalanced and fell on the bed, his bulk grinding into my bones, I'd arch my back like a gymnast, but whether to dislodge him or to feel him more keenly, I couldn't say.

Fuck, fight, and flight: states of arousal. I imagine that the neural pathways are pretty much the same.

PLEASE NOTE—AGAIN this is no time for false modesty—that I am in many ways an accomplished woman. I'm a highly competent immigration attorney, a skilled amateur violinist, a fair-to-middling squash player, a reluctant but talented cook. I am, if I say so myself, well read, well traveled, well dressed. I speak four languages and have become something of an expert on antique maps and prints. But I have never—*never*—claimed any expertise in the area of human intimacy.

Ask Tom. In this domain, I suggest you depose Tom.

Tom and I shared an apartment while I was in law school and he was at the School of Public Health, doing research that consisted, as far as I could tell, of putting rats' brains through the blender. He was a lean, serious farm boy from the South, thrifty and intelligent-fingered, not exactly a live wire, but handy to have around the house. He taught me how to use my first Macintosh. He taught me how to set the timing on my VW Bug. He taught me how to grow Hungarian wax peppers in a flower-pot on the porch. He was my friend, my handy man, and, for three years, I suppose, my lover as well.

"Some other time," I'd demurred when he first raised the subject, unusually bold after a few shots of Wild Turkey. But being a scientist and literal-minded, he'd asked "When?"

Somehow, after that, it seemed too complicated to back out.

MYSTERY BOYFRIEND COMES FORWARD IN CHANDLER CASE
Boston Globe, January 5, 1995

Stating that he could no longer tolerate the media harassment, the "mystery boyfriend" in the Christine Chandler case—the man with whom she shared a Cambridge apartment for three years—has stepped forward to reveal his identity. He is Dr. Thomas P. Painter, an associate professor of microbiology at the Harvard School of Public Health. Speaking from his Longwood Avenue laboratory yesterday, Painter said, "I can no longer cope with the constant interruptions to my work and the invasions of my family's privacy. As a preemptive measure, I have decided to identify myself and to state publicly what little I know on the subject of Christine Chandler. Then, perhaps, this absurd storm of attention will blow over and I can get on with my life. And, of course, with my research, which, may I remind you, is partially funded by the taxpayer."

Reading from a prepared statement, Painter continued: "Christine Chandler and I were roommates between 1981 and 1984, when we shared a Harvard-owned apartment on Kirkland Street. I was, at the time, a graduate student in microbiology, and she had recently moved to Cambridge to begin her studies at Harvard Law. Ms. Chandler answered an ad that I had posted at the housing office, seeking a roommate, and, since she seemed like a responsible, congenial person, I invited her to move in.

"Discovering that we were, indeed, compatible, we shared the same apartment for the next three years, maintaining separate lives, separate bedrooms, and separate bank accounts. Since we were both working extremely long hours, we saw relatively little of each other on a daily basis. But, largely by reason of proximity, we became, as the media have suggested, intimate on occasion. I saw no signs of violence or abnormality in Ms. Chandler's behavior at the time.

"In 1984, I decided to move to Brookline, which was more convenient to my laboratory at the School of Public Health. My relations with Ms. Chandler remained cordial, though, naturally, over time, they waned. I am now married with two fine children, I have not seen Ms. Chandler in at least eight years, and I have absolutely no knowledge of her private life. I was as shocked as anyone to hear of her arrest, and I implore the media to respect my family's privacy and my own. There will be no further comment. Thank you."

When Tom announced that he was moving out, he said it was to be closer to his lab. But I believe, in retrospect, that it was to be further from me—to put the Charles River between us, to translate into topographical terms the distance that had grown between us. The distance that, I see now, he'd been trying all along to bridge.

He moved in with someone else a year or so later, a nice technician from his lab.

Much to my surprise, I'd been alone ever since.

I still called Tom on his birthday and whenever my computer did something I didn't understand. Sometimes it froze. At other times, possessed by some demon, it would eat up my text and spew out terrifying hieroglyphics, unintelligible typographical taunts.

TO RETURN, HOWEVER, to the topic at hand: the flowers and tea, the tenderness, lasted only a week or so, and, thereafter, our relations headed straight for hell. As, of course, anyone but the defendant could have foreseen.

We'd been out to dinner, I forget where, and had begun to argue, I forget why—nothing in particular, Patty perhaps. After a while, he turned mute, his usual ploy, and sat staring somewhere west of his plate, pushing food into his squared-off mouth like mail into a slot.

Nor did he say a word on the way home. Hunched over the wheel, he drove with murderous speed, running red lights and jockeying against cabs, while I shrank against the unforgiving arm of the door. As we approached my block, he didn't, as usual, slow down to scavenge for a parking place; instead he sped up, screeching to a halt next to a double-parked van.

I unbuckled my seatbelt, unlocked the door, creaked it open a crack, then, don't ask me why, turned to him and said "Come on up."

"It's late," he said, staring straight ahead.

"Please," I said.

He didn't respond.

"Please come." No answer. "Come up*stairs,*" I repeated, my face flaming alive.

"Chris," he said, without turning his head, revving the idle to emphasize his point, "I'm going home."

"Fine," I replied, slamming the door shut and rebuckling my belt. "I'll come too."

Not the smartest move, I grant you: I should have salvaged my scant remaining self-respect and sent him home. *I* know that. *You* know that. But, really, what difference does it make what we know now? My body was flooded with the raw chemicals of fear, which are, you'll agree, rarely conducive to ratiocination. When he refused to look at me, refused to see me, when he canceled me out like that, a wild and choking panic surged up my throat, and that was it.

So that's how I ended up back at his place, the primal scene. He didn't acknowledge my presence in the car, true, but neither did he do anything to prevent me from following him up the echoey steps. He didn't invite me to sit down, true, but neither did he prevent me from doing so when he himself did, slouching on the scarred black sofa, sucking vodka from a paper cup. Riffling through a back issue of *Things*, he refused to meet my eye. I poured myself a vodka too, why not, and pretended to study yesterday's front page, "Bludgeoned Female Corpse."

"This is absurd," I said, after a while.

"What is?" he replied, without raising his eyes.

"Us sitting here like this. Not talking."

"What's there to talk about?" He turned a page with unnecessary force.

"Oh, I don't know," I said, heat rising again in my face. "You. Me. And"—out it surged, in a vengeful flash—"items of female lingerie that might be squirreled away in your closet. Your pathetic little fetishes. Your lies."

That got his attention. He shot upright, leapt to his feet, and, with strawberry-colored blotches spreading across face and neck, demanded to know what the hell I was talking about. Since I could hardly admit the extent of my evidence-gathering activities, I offered an abridged version, establishing merely that he had underestimated my access not only to his closets but to his squalid little mind. I wasn't exactly an idiot, I told him, and neither, he retorted, was he, though I always fucking treated him like one, didn't I. Be that as it may, I continued—raising one palm to silence him—he couldn't be trusted, both of us knew that, nor, and this was the truly pathetic part, was he smart enough to cover his tracks. That's when he began to yell—how dare I, and so on.

"What gives you the right?" he kept saying. "This is *my* goddamn house. I'll do whatever I like in my own goddamn house. I'll keep whatever I like in my own goddamn closets, too, thank you very much. It's none of your fucking business. I just can't believe you'd have the nerve."

When I retorted that that was hardly the point, he asked what was.

"The point is," I began, but he cut me off, like a knife: "And who the hell ever asked you to come here, anyway, in the first place?"

"*You* did," I replied, springing likewise to my feet and facing him, eye to eye, across the coffee table—though at that moment I couldn't recall a single instance when he'd actually invited me; we'd just sort of ended up there, as couples do. "I'll come here whenever I like," I continued, asserting a right, "and I'll look in whatever the hell closets I like, too." Fair warning, as we say in the legal trade. "What makes you think you can stop me?"

I saw what was going to happen next a split second before it did. He lunged towards me, forgetting the low table between us, cracked his shin, lost his balance, thrashed at the air to regain it, and, thrashing, caught me smack across the nose with his right fist. There was a stunned, blank moment during which my whole face seemed to flatten out, numb and glassy as a windshield—and then came the insult of pain everywhere at once, nose, cheekbones, eyes, temples, skull, throat. Something hot and thick, too, which I thought was snot but turned out to be blood.

It stained his white T-shirt as he held me to him, trembling, whimpering, stroking my hair, asking over and over what he should do, swearing it had been an accident, that he hadn't meant it, that it would never happen again—never, ever, ever. I leaned limply against him, trembling too, until the bleeding stopped, but later, as I wept in his arms, it started again. He bathed my face tenderly with a warm cloth and at that moment, even before we made love, I understood something for the first time: the one who causes the pain is the one who must cure it.

I TOLD ROSA, and my clients, and anyone else who asked, that I'd had an accident on the squash court. Squash, as everyone knows, is a very dangerous game.

This doesn't mean, however, that I'm planning to plead battered woman syndrome, though I think my legal team might still be tempted by that recourse. Who would believe it, anyway—that a twenty-six-year-old boy could have held me in his thrall? The very idea would be laughed out of court. And, anyway, that's not the way it was. He may have acted roughly on occasion, yes, but I see quite clearly how I provoked it, how the situation as a whole provoked it. I'm not so naive that I don't understand what we were doing, how we were playing with sex and power. I gave up power in bed, or pretended to, as a game—as a way, perhaps, of having more. Sometimes he forgot that it was a game. Sometimes I did. That's all.

BEFORE I GO any further, I want to make it clear that he never hit me again. In the face, I mean. I wouldn't have stood for that. Yes, there was one night, in the car, right near the end . . . but that was, technically, a slap, and I slapped him right back. That should have been the end of that. Except that, a few seconds later, I discovered that the earring on that side, a diamond stud, had fallen out. Or been knocked out, whatever. So, as he drove on, I doubled over and fumbled for it under the seat. Nasty oily springs, gritty rubber mat, hairy curve of

center console, but no earring. I gave up and began
to unbend, at which moment he swung the car
around a corner so fiercely that the back of my skull
knocked, *thwack,* on the underside of the dash. It
was an accident, of course: he couldn't have cho-
reographed it if he'd tried. Nevertheless, at that moment it seemed too much to bear.

OVER THE NEXT few weeks, I tried, believe me, to get
a grip on my life, to stem the chaos that was fester-
ing around me. My apartment had become, by degrees, unlivable: making a list, I found that I
needed groceries, clean clothes, toilet paper, and
soap; I needed to retrieve most of my pantyhose
from under the bed, sweep the crumbs and mop the
splotches from the kitchen floor, scrub the scum off
the bathtub, wipe the city soot from the window
seat, empty the trash. I needed a new lightbulb to
replace the burnt-out case in the hall. I needed to
pay some bills and balance my accounts, wash a
sinkful of scabby dishes, take my shoes to Mr. Wu
for new soles. I also needed to return about a
month's worth of calls.

Let the record show that I did in fact try to return
those calls, in each instance without success. An-

gelica had left for Jamaica in a concert promoter's jet, her roommate said; Steph was in the lab till all hours, trying to get her viruses to replicate before their grant money ran out; and Julie, I forget where Julie was—at a conference in Montreal, I think (you could check with her assistant, Brett). As I'm sure you know, if you neglect your friends for a month or two, they don't conveniently rematerialize just when you need them. Even the AIDS hotline, which I wished to consult about a blotch on my wrist, had closed down for lack of funds.

I did, however, reach my parents in Marin County one Sunday afternoon, informing them, as usual, that I was fine, that work was fine, that the weather, too, was fine. They were fine as well.

Family, I thought, as I hung up: a group of people connected by lies.

I mention this, by the way, not to suggest, as is currently the vogue, that my parents are to blame for my pathology—though, come to think of it, they may well be—nor even to dredge up some rancid memory of childhood abuse. Anyone hoping for such an explanation is out of luck: my parents, both corporate lawyers, wouldn't have had the time to abuse me even if they'd wanted to. No, I simply want to establish my state of mind, my self-imposed quarantine.

The talk-show pundits have been asking each other, with furrowed brows, why I didn't let anyone know what was going on before things got out of hand, why I didn't, as they say, "come forward"—as if "coming forward" were such a simple, self-evident act. They can't imagine what it feels like to become, by degrees, helpless and mute, as if you were the last person left in your own life, as if your life were a bombed building from which everyone else had long since found the way out.

I don't mean to sound melodramatic. I just can't think how else to put it.

I WOULD, HOWEVER, like to point out—because it matters to me—that, during all this disarray, my performance at work remained impeccable. I doubt that anyone at Weisner, Bickey, & Taft even knew I had a private life, much less that it was in such an alarming state. (They know now, of course.) Regardless of what might have happened the night before, I arrived at the office every morning by eight and stayed, every evening, until seven at least. Except for an occasional lapse in concentration while

meeting with a client—which could happen to anyone—I functioned at a very high level of efficiency,
if I do say so myself; in fact, I found it a relief to
focus on something I could understand, sentences
and situations that were perfectly clear. *Pursuant to
8 CFR.2 (a)(4)(ii), if your application for adjustment of status is denied, you will be subject to exclu-
sion proceedings under Section 236,* and so on. Only
once did the chaos reach through my office door,
and that was the day Scott showed up impersonat-
ing a delivery boy—but I'll get to that.

The nights, which no-one knew about, were a
different kettle of hell. I hadn't been sleeping well
for some time—bad dreams and such—but then a
new malady began: I would wake up in the dark,
dying. That was the only explanation that occurred
to me: I was dying, my heart was attacking me, I
would never be able to fill my lungs again, and I
would die. I would die there alone, sooner or later a
neighbor would notice the smell, but in the meanwhile my throat wouldn't open, I couldn't suck
down any air, I was choking and wheezing, I
couldn't even gasp: help, I wanted to gasp, SOS,
emergency, oxygen please: mom, dad, ambulance, a
crab of harsh pain has its claws in my chest; pin-

points of light popping like flashbulbs in the dark; any second now there'll be a knock-out, fade-out, black-out, if I don't just breathe, just breathe, just open my throat and haul in some air.

I never mentioned this to my doctor, in case she said it was fatal or worse, and, as usual, the *Home Medical Cyclopedia* could offer no help. *Heart attack* wasn't listed, nor was *-break* or *-ache; cardiac arrest* was, but I knew that my heart hadn't yet ceased to beat. My symptoms were dispersed under various ills: "severe paroxysmal pain" under *angina,* "air hunger" under *dyspnea,* and, under *myocarditis,* "an enlarged and greatly scarred heart." But the best match, I thought, was *heartshake,* which affects only trees.

Heartshake, *n. (also* **starshake***):* in a piece of timber, a radial shake caused by inadequate seasoning or decay at the center.

Sometime in September, I forget the exact date, I invited him out to dinner—a small celebration, a minor victory over the Immigration and Naturalization Service, nothing a non-lawyer would appreciate, but, to me, worth a few bucks and a bottle of champagne. I even gave Rosa a bouquet of blue irises and the afternoon off. But when I called Scott around three to remind him I'd swing by at eight, he said—sounding hoarse and bleary and none too celebratory—that he didn't really feel like going anywhere after all, thanks. He'd been up the whole night, he claimed, covering an opening at the ICA and then working in the darkroom till dawn. Like hell, I thought, never having known him to exert himself on deadline for *Things*.

"Last-minute panic," he said. "Robert didn't even give me the tickets until five-fifteen, and then . . ."

"Well," I said, feeling a tiny mobile twinge in my chest, like a run in my hose, "how about an early dinner at my place, then, if going to Olives would be too much of a scene?"

"Chris," he said, "I'm really . . ."

"Come on," I coaxed. "It'll be fun. I'll try to get home at a reasonable hour"—which I did, six or thereabouts, plenty of time to cook and bathe. I made gazpacho from the last fruits of Steph's garden, I wore the silky grey dress with nothing underneath, I opened a bottle of Rioja—most of which I later knocked back by myself.

He showed up later than he'd said he would and

immediately clicked on the TV to catch the tail end of the news. Five minutes later, when I brought in the wine and warm goat cheese, he was stretched out on the rug like a corpse—fast asleep, head canted against the couch. Canned laughter yapped out from the TV, and its busy blue light licked his face, disfiguring it. As I stood over him, I felt the same unnerving sensation that I'd felt once or twice before: the conviction that I had never set eyes on this person, that there was a foreign body in the room.

"Scott?" I said, becoming, I don't know why, alarmed. "Scott?" I repeated, prodding him with my toe. I eased the remote control from his hand and zapped the pandemonium to its vanishing point, but he didn't move. I called his name again. I shook him, hard, and then he woke.

"What?" he muttered, as he always did when startled awake, rubbing his raspy hair as if he had no idea where he was. "Oh," he said, blinking me into focus. "Sorry, Chris. Guess I really should have stayed home tonight."

"Want to eat something and go straight to bed, then?" I asked.

"No," he said, "I'm, like, totally wiped out. Just let me sleep and I'll be fine." He staggered up and into the bedroom where, removing his shoes, he collapsed. Not knowing what to feel—which would be more reasonable under the circumstances, resentment or forbearance?—I did all the things that, in the movies, people do when the dinner is abandoned, the celebration cut short. I cleared the table and put the food into plastic containers. I ate a few spoonfuls of flan straight out of the dish. I blew out the candles on the mantelpiece. I sat on the window seat and finished the wine. Then, undressing in the bathroom and finding my way in the dark—so as not to disturb him and, frankly, not to have to deal with him at all—I joined him. He lay sprawled on the quilt, but I slipped under it, in the taut remaining pocket of space. It was, after all, my bed; I had nowhere else to go.

What happened next is a matter of some dispute, though it shouldn't be: I recall it with suffocating clarity. I woke up in the middle of the night to find him lying with his full weight across my chest, forearm flung across my throat, choking me. I flailed. He pressed. I coughed, flailed again, and dug my fingernails deep into the flesh of his arm. He snatched his arm away and, fumbling blindly at the bedside table, found the switch on the base of the lamp.

"What the hell . . . ?" he asked, looking, in the

sudden dazzle, disoriented and afraid. "Why the hell were you attacking me like that?"

Why, in other words, was *I* attacking *him*. He claimed, and claims to this day, that he woke up in the middle of the night confused, fully dressed, not knowing where he was or even that there was another body in the bed; he claims too that, if he did somehow roll onto me, it was an accident. He also had the nerve to say that people often wake up with a feeling of suffocation—a common physiological phenomenon, he informed me (his dad is a doctor, so he thinks he's one too). He claimed, and claims to this day, that it was he who woke up to find me attacking him, unprovoked. I asked him then, and I ask you now: how likely is that?

AT TIMES, I grant you, I may have overreacted—or maybe not: I'm too exhausted, too confused, to know the difference any more. Let me just say that lack of trust is like a virus: once it's entered the system, it amplifies. The Ebola virus, for instance, which destroys the body from within, eating the connective tissue and clotting the blood, until, one by one, the vital organs die. Eventually, of course, the skin bursts, and the body, as they say, "bleeds out." I apologize if this analogy seems grotesque (my lawyer says it's irrelevant, too), but all I'm trying to do is establish the defendant's state of mind—which was, you'll agree, beginning to fray.

Take, for instance, one evening when I hadn't seen him for a week—work, he said—and he showed up forty minutes late, double-parking and beeping impatiently outside my door. Determined, nonetheless, to be cheery, I climbed into the car, said "Hi, sweetie" (I called Rosa sweetie too, so it didn't count), leaned back, reached for the seatbelt, and, in a sudden swoop, felt the backrest give way, tipping me smartly to a supine position. I don't know if that's ever happened to you, but it's an unnerving sensation, akin, I imagine, to dropping off the edge of the earth. Dazed, I stared at the ceiling for a few seconds, discovering a small galaxy of pinholes in the plastic overhead. Then I struggled gracelessly upright, fumbling beside me for the adjustment knob.

"Who's been sitting in *my* seat?" I asked, doing Baby Bear.

"Nobody," he said. "Nobody's been in the car."

"Right," I teased. "It just decided to do that by itself, I suppose." I knew, with a pang, that it hadn't, because one night he'd parked his car on the bank of the Charles, tuned the radio to a country-music station, and, with the skyline wavering in the dark water below us, struggled to flip back the seat so we could have sex.

"Nobody's been in the car," he repeated, unamused.

"Well," I joked, "then there must be something wrong with your . . . knob."

"Who would've been in the car?" he asked, not listening to me. "I've spent the entire week on assignment, working like a dog. Maybe I flipped it back to fit some of my stuff in the front seat, I honestly don't remember. Anyway, what the fuck does it matter?"

"It's OK," I said, becoming a little alarmed. "Only kidding."

"That's what you always say," he muttered, "but you never are." His lower lip squared off and his shoulders slumped. He lit a cigarette and held it so that the smoke streamed into my eyes as he drove.

Maybe I was being a little unreasonable. Maybe he was. Odds are that we both were. But being unreasonable isn't a crime yet—fortunately—nor is not always being nice.

* * *

INTERPERSONAL RELATIONS WOULD be so much simpler, I've always thought, if you could just wheel a polygraph out of the closet, attach its sensors to your dinner guest, and apply, at will, the Control Question Technique, the Guilty Knowledge Test. But you can't, of course. Hence the vertigo, the soul-sickness, of doubt.

I once saw a picture of an experiment in which a scientist had coaxed a kitten, cringing and flat-eared, across a mirrored floor. As soon as the poor creature looked down, it couldn't move: it thought the world beneath its feet had fled.

That's what I mean by the vertigo of doubt.

What, after all, did I know about this man, this boy, who'd found his way so deeply into me? I knew his name, address, and date of birth, since I'd seen them on his driver's license—but what kind of knowledge was that? I knew the color of his eyes—blue, green, or sea-grey, depending on the light—but what kind of knowledge was that? I knew where he worked. I knew what kind of car he drove. I knew which toothpaste he preferred. I knew that apricots and plums were his favorite fruits. I knew the musk of his skin, the flush of his face, the weight of his flesh. I knew which touch of my tongue, where, would make him gasp. But what kind of knowledge was that?

I knew, too, that this was a most effective way to drive myself insane, like staring at the stars or repeating, over and over, a single word. Word. Word. Word. Nevertheless, I couldn't stop. If that is the definition of insanity—to be unable to stop yourself from doing something you know is insane—then I hereby plead guilty: look no further, bring on the chlorpromazine, hospitalize me for life, watch me grow thick and wasted and wan at taxpayers' expense. But perhaps—have you considered this— sanity might consist precisely in knowing the difference, in knowing which of your actions are sane and which are not. And, at that stage, I was still capable of making such distinctions.

For instance, I did not, as has been reported, "repeatedly" search the complainant's place of residence—once was quite enough—nor did I "break in" in order to do so. I didn't have to. I knew where he kept a key.

He kept a spare key by the downstairs door, in a wooden flower tub, where the pansies, battered by a recent rain, bowed their heads as if puking over the edge. I felt like puking myself as I dug for the key, though I knew, having dropped him at the station, that he was safely en route to New York. I'd wanted to join him—it was a weekend trip—but he'd changed his plans at the last moment, don't remember why.

I didn't know what I was looking for, but I wanted to see everything: his canceled checks, his phone bill, his credit-card slips, his car payments, his Videosmith card, his laundry bag. Everyone is guilty of something, I reasoned—in my case, unwarranted search and seizure—and if I looked hard enough, I might find out what. Just as, if I peered into your bathroom cabinet or bedside drawer, I might find something you wouldn't want mentioned in a court of law. Mightn't I.

He had athlete's foot, I discovered, not really a crime. Prescriptions for pain—back pain, headache pain, neck pain. He had miniature shampoos from a Florida hotel. He had remedies for indigestion, depression, motion sickness, and hives. Well, so did I, except for the hives.

From the hall table I stole back a book I'd given him but that he hadn't bothered to read, Rilke's *Letters to a Young Poet*. I can't imagine, now, why I ever thought he would.

From his desk I scooped up a few bills to audit at

my leisure: he never paid them anyway, so what difference would it make?

In the kitchen, I found five coffee-stained mugs, an embarrassment of evidence, unless I was looking to convict him of caffeine abuse. None, to my relief—or rather, to my strange disappointment—was lipstick-stained. I paused to flip open the trash bin with my foot, but just as I was about to investigate a promising-looking fax, I heard what sounded like footsteps at the door, someone stopping outside to grope for a key. I froze in a rictus of panic, then, heart skittering, heard the noise again, and this time it sounded like what it was, a car door slamming in the distance. By the time my heart had slowed down, I was ready to leave.

That was it. I lost my nerve. I didn't even make it to the bedroom this time—much less derange his drawers, as has been alleged. How would he have known anyway, since they were always, let's face it, such a godawful mess? And, more to the point, why should I lie about this, having already confessed so much?

I did, I admit, search his wallet a couple of times while he was in the shower. He left it lying in plain sight, after all; if you leave things where people can look at them, they will. Basic primate behavior, I

would say. By studying his ATM slips, I discovered
that he had even less money in the bank than I'd
suspected; I also found a recent receipt from Angelica's bar, a scrap of paper with a New York address,
an ancient but intact condom, a card illustrating
CPR technique, and a photo of Patty. Grinning her
head off, as well she might.

In the legal profession, we call it information
gathering. He, however, called it *stalking*.

DEPOSITION OF STEPHANIE MADELEINE
RYAN, M.D., Ph.D.
Senior Staff Scientist, RepliCo Inc.
Cambridge, Massachusetts
February 14, 1995

Ms. Katz, I'm afraid there isn't very much I
can tell you. For one thing, I never met Scott,
and, for another, Christine never confided in me
about this relationship. She never confided in
anyone about anything, really.

But I would like to say this, for the record.
I've known Chris for over ten years—we met
through her roommate, Tom, when we were
both in grad school—and it's my impression
that she has been a very lonely person and, in
my opinion, quite possibly clinically depressed
most of her life. I also think that she drinks too
much, in an attempt to self-medicate, and that
that's a big part of the problem.

I know this next thing will sound odd,

because in some ways Chris seems so
sophisticated, but I really do believe that she's
somewhat naive about sex. Not inexperienced,
that's not what I mean—but more that, when
she talks about it, it all sounds very abstract,
as if there's something about it that she
fundamentally *doesn't get*. I'm not even sure
that she likes men or sex that much; she just
doesn't strike me as a particularly physical
person, as, you know, a passionate person.
That's why, in a strange way, this horrible
thing didn't really surprise me—not that I saw
it coming, no, no-one did, but, once it had
happened, I thought: well, *yes*. It seemed to
make some kind of sense.

I'd also like to add that, despite everything, I
think Chris is basically a decent human being,
which most people seem to have lost sight of.
That's why I'm standing by her, why I offered
her the cabin in Vermont when she got out of
McLean, the way I'd stand by any friend
who's in trouble.

I've thought about this carefully, and I
believe that's really all I have to say on the
subject. Thank you very much. Let me know if
I can be of any further assistance.

One evening he dragged me by the hair into his
car on Commonwealth Avenue. I mention this because a travesty of this incident has already appeared in a magazine—probably from the same
tainted source, Mrs. Jean Malloy, who will, it

seems, say anything for gin money. I mention it too because it was the last time I saw Scott—in person, I mean, in the flesh—before the night of the assault. Alleged assault, whatever you want to call it.

That evening—chilly, with a chip of early moon—I trudged home from work with a heavy briefcase and a spasm in my shoulder blade, fretting about a call I'd forgotten to return, an I-91 that Rosa hadn't received in time. So I didn't see him sitting outside my building in the dark, on a low wall partly overgrown by a lilac bush; didn't notice the red eye of his cigarette. He waited till I had almost passed him and then called out my name, startling me.

"Scott," I said, exhaling in relief, "you gave me a fright."

"I meant to," he replied, moving into the dim light of the street lamp. "You looked like such a *lawyer*, scurrying along there."

"What do you mean, such a *lawyer?*"

"In your little suit, with your little briefcase, staring at the ground." And here he performed a few steps in mimicry, bunching his brow into a worried frown.

"Yeah well," I said. "It's been a long day."

"Anyway," he said, dropping the pantomime, "I've come to abduct you."

"I don't think so," I said. "I'm tired. I've had a rough day. And I still have work to do for tomorrow."

"You're not the only one who's had a rough day, lawyer-girl," he said, kicking the base of the lamppost with small, vandalistic scuffs. "I think Robert's about ready to fire me." Tension between Scott and Robert, the two-person photo department of *Things*, erupted reliably every couple of months or so, or whenever deadlines were tight. It subsided, just as reliably, within a few days, though neither of them ever seemed to remember that at the time.

"Uh-oh," I said. "Not again. Want to go over to Davio's and get a drink, then?" I turned back towards Newbury Street, the direction from which I'd just come, resigned to spending a couple of hours with him since I could see he was upset.

"I've already had a drink," he said, "or three," which appeared to be an understatement. "I've come to abduct you."

"What do you mean, *abduct?*"

"Take you away in my car for a drive." He liked to drive, fast and dangerously, without destination, when his mood turned dark. (As you know: you've already heard the thwack.)

"Sorry," I replied, fishing in my briefcase for my keys. "I don't think I'm up for being abducted tonight. I'll have a drink and some dinner with you, but that's about it."

He was silent for a second or two, then, with a sudden sideways swipe, knocked the keys out of my hand, into the lilac bush, into the dark.

"That's not funny," I said, losing patience. "Now help me look for them."

"No," he said. "I want you to get in the car with me."

"Look," I said, bending over to fumble in the flower bed, encountering odd damp lumps and scratchy things, "this isn't funny, OK? I'm not in the mood for this at all." I straightened up exasperated, empty-handed.

"I don't care what you're in the mood for," he said quietly, stepping up behind me and grasping my hair. "You're coming with me." And in that manner he tugged me backwards towards the car.

Before you conjure up every caveman cartoon you've ever seen, please note that he wasn't actually *dragging* me by the hair; he was just tugging, insistently, in such a manner that it made more sense, caused less pain, to stagger backwards than to stay put.

Yes, I could have screamed and fought, made a scene—if he'd been a stranger that's what I would have done, adding a few sharp kicks to groin and knee for good measure. But instead—I don't quite know how to explain this—instead, as he tugged me the few feet to the curb, I prayed that no-one would hear, no-one would see. Perhaps it was because I hoped it might yet prove to be a game. (As, to this day, he claims it was.) Perhaps it was because I was afraid he might hurt me. Or perhaps it was, quite simply, because the spectacle was too humiliating: a woman in high heels and a business suit, briefcase still in hand, being tugged backwards by the hair over the cobblestones of Commonwealth Avenue, in imminent danger of losing her balance.

My point, you see, is this: I could have stopped him if I'd tried hard enough. But I didn't.

MY LAWYER WANTS to know what happened once we got into the complainant's car. I don't remember, I tell her—we just drove around, I suppose. I lost an earring, that I do recall.

And then? she asks. And then, I suppose, we drove back to Back Bay and found a parking spot. He must have helped me find my keys under the lilac bush—or maybe he didn't, maybe I did that myself the next day. And, yes, he spent the night.

It's very hard for me to admit that; I've asked myself so often, with such deep shame, why I didn't send him packing, why I—meekly, sheepishly—followed him up my own stairs to my own bed. All I can say, and I offer this not as an excuse but as an observation, is that, after having been abraded in some way, body or soul, a person might crave solace, the way a child with a grazed knee might crave a salve—and, sometimes, the abrader is the only one around to offer it.

In other words, I suppose, I don't know; can't explain.

But I do know this much: I don't enjoy pain. Nobody does. What I enjoy, obviously, is sensation; that's how you know you're alive, that you haven't retreated so far inside yourself that no-one will ever be able to find you again.

And that night he hurt me. Caused real pain. Physical pain, of the dry searing kind. He said things to me, ugly things, and he shoved me face-down into the panicky dark of the pillow. When I made a sound, he clamped his hand over my jaw until I tasted salt—his sweat, my blood. He used his full body weight, twice mine, to keep me down. Then something slammed into my coccyx, his knee I think, and I knew, in a sharp flare of distress, that this wasn't a game.

As the entire tabloid-reading population of the United States knows by now, we had, on occasion, used handcuffs and such, mainly as *mise-en-scène*, mainly for him, reared as he'd been on MTV. But this time was different. Blood was involved; pain. A sex crime was committed. I don't mean to sound coy, believe me—how on earth would that help my case?—but I don't see that every abject detail is relevant. Nor do I, to be frank, recall them all. Everything happened so fast, and I could barely breathe. What I do remember is the pain—pain, and some bitter rageful sense of, I don't know quite what to call it. Desolation.

I don't know why it happened that night and not another, why not the previous week or the following full moon. I don't know—simple as that. You may as well ask a virus on what day, exactly, it's planning to shut down the spleen.

This is what matters, though, this is my point: that, by the end of that night, something had given way inside me, with a dull broken twang, and I knew that, whatever he might do or say, I would never allow him near me again.

As he rushed out to his car the next morning, trying to beat the meter maid who always showed up at one minute past eight, he forgot to yell "Bye" until he was almost through the door.

"Bye," I replied, stepping out of the bathroom to watch him go, blurrily, since I had only one contact lens in, the other poised on a fingertip. "And if you ever come back here again, believe me, I'll rip your eyes out."

Then, quite calmly, I double-locked the door.

THAT SHOULD HAVE been the end of it, right there, at 8:02 A.M. on October the 11th. And, in a way, that was the end. What happened later, the deed itself, was, in a sense, superfluous. Oh, I don't mean that the way it sounds, that it lacked significance, far from it, I mean . . . how can I put it? I mean that, in some essential way, the damage had already been done.

5

The next day I changed my telephone number to
an unlisted one. Obscene caller, I told the phone
company—ironically enough, in light of what was to
come. I signed up for a women's self-defense class
that met at my gym, Wednesdays from six to nine. I
made an appointment with Julie's psychiatrist in
Newton. In other words, I took charge of the situation.

Why, then, my lawyer wants to know, didn't
I change the locks on my door? Simple: I didn't
know that he had a key. But, she says, Christine,
really, as you well know, he claims you gave it
to him yourself. Yeah right, I reply: does that
seem like something I would do? Ask any of my
other gentleman callers if I ever gave *them*
a key; I've always insisted on knowing exactly
who I'm letting in: it's the first law of urban survival.

Other laws of urban survival: look both ways

before crossing the road, don't talk to strangers, don't take sweets from strangers, don't get into cars with strange men. Carry a condom at all times. It's confusing, living amongst strangers. Some strangers, you discover, are stranger than others.

In the self-defense class, we were advised to assume that any male human being might wish to harm us. Our goal, the instructor told us, was to harm him back, or, better still, to harm him first. Standing in a circle—eight assorted women and our coach, a small, compact kick boxer with brawny forearms—we first had to learn how to yell, to produce large hoarse bellows of anger and aggression. This, apparently, is difficult for women to do. Then we had to learn how to hit. With all our strength, without holding back, with genuine intent to hurt. Then we had to learn where the vulnerable spots are, how to fight quick and dirty like the playground runt—a kick to the kneecap, elbow in the gullet, surprise blow to the crotch, and, no squeamishness allowed, fingers in the eyes.

(Let me point out, parenthetically, that I'm of squeamish disposition. I don't like to swim in the sea, for instance, because there are too many un-

identified slimy objects in there; I can hardly bear
to look at a raw chicken or to reach my hand, if
need be, into the oozy pulp of the garbage disposal.
And once, having accidentally drowned a spider,
I'm not exaggerating, I retched.)

BACK BAY TRAINING
SD 101: "Self-Defense and Street Safety for Women"
Instructor: Marta Tereshkova

Lesson One.

Welcome! By the time you leave here, you will
feel a lot more confident about your ability to
defend yourself against any attacker. Remember, your assailant is likely to have the advan-
tage in size and strength, but you can learn to
fight back with strategic strikes to the least protected parts of his body.

Most women are understandably squeamish
about the idea of hurting another person, but
consider the following:

• In over 80% of rapes reported to the police,
the assailants were able to intimidate their vic-
tims with verbal threats alone.

• The average attacker is not some huge monster, but stands only 5′ 8″ tall, weighing 150 lbs.

• The vast majority of all violence against
women takes place not in parking lots, alleys, or
public rest rooms, but in the woman's home.

• Over 75% of sexual assaults occur at the
hands of someone the victim knows.

If you're going to fight, it's best to fight early,
before your attacker gets momentum going. To

do this, you must use instantly debilitating techniques on the least protected targets. Primary
targets for hand strikes, in order of importance,
are:

1. eyes
2. throat
3. groin
4. elbows

<u>A Note of Caution:</u> when you go into the adren-
aline state necessary to fend off an attacker,
your body will undergo a number of physiological changes, one of which may be tunnel vision—the loss of your ability to see peripherally.
Be aware, then, that in an emergency, you
might not perceive everything that is happening
around you.

Remember, the more prepared you are to defend yourself, the less likely it is you will ever
have to do it.

Learn to think like a warrior! Plan and practice at every opportunity!

After we'd rehearsed our gouging and throttling
techniques for a while, the instructor presented us
with a man to practice on, blank and padded like
the Michelin Man. He stood patiently, domestically,
while we re-formed our circle about him. And he
continued to stand as we fell upon him one by one
with throaty cries, aiming, as instructed, for his

knees and eyes. I tried to see his face before I attacked him, but couldn't, under its protective mask, and, though I kicked his knee pads with aplomb, I felt absurd, unclean, as if assaulting a balloon at the Thanksgiving parade. Why had he gone into this line of work, I wondered—to expiate what crime? And, I wondered as I launched myself towards him, what kind of power is this?

I didn't go back the following Wednesday. Nor did I keep the doctor's appointment in Newton. Something came up, I forget what.

DEPOSITION OF ANGELICA RICHMOND
Co-proprietor, Bar Lethe, Prague
Per telephone
February 27, 1995

Hello? Hello? Can you hear me? Sorry? I'm not hearing you too well, all I hear is my own voice echoing back, which is kind of distracting. And this phone line could cut out at any moment, which they tend to do around here, so we should try to get this thing done as quickly as possible.

What? Yeah, I know—sorry it took you so long to track me down. It was kind of a sudden move. If I'd known you were trying to get in touch with me . . . But tell me, Laurie,

how is Chris? *Where* is she? Look, honey, I'm
on the other side of the planet, what difference
could it make? OK, if you can't, you can't.
Please send her my love, anyway, tell her
Prague is a really cool city and she has to
come and see my new bar.

Someday, I mean.

OK, so what can I tell you? Mmn-hmn. Sure.
Sure, I'll confirm that: she met Scott at my
place, at New Year's, so I feel kind of
responsible for the whole thing, though I *never*
thought Chris would go for him, it just never
even crossed my mind. I thought it was kind
of humorous at first, the way she got
obliterated on vodka and dragged this cute
boy home, totally out of character, like she'd
decided to begin making up for lost time in a
big way. And he was cute, no mistake about
that—I even fucked him myself once, months
before Chris met him, just a one-night thing,
you know, some night when he was hanging
around the bar at closing time. Sometimes
we'd have lunch together, too, when we were
both doing work at *Things* and needed to get
the hell out of there for a while. Cute boy,
really cute, but kind of moody, I thought.

Sorry, didn't hear that? Oh, OK—no, she
didn't really talk about it, but every now and
then she'd say something that made me feel
she might be getting in over her head. At first
I thought it was a great idea for her to hang
out with Scott, kick loose, have some fun for a
change, but later she said some things—I wish

I could remember exactly what they were—
that made me wonder what exactly was going
on between them. Whether things were getting
too intense, you know.

No, I didn't say anything at the time: I
mean, first of all, I'm not really the one to be
going around telling people to restrain
themselves, and second of all, Chris wasn't
looking for advice. She was just talking,
thinking out loud, drinking: she'd only say
stuff like this when she'd been drinking. She'd
say a lot of weird stuff then—stuff about her
and Scott that I didn't believe for a minute,
like how they'd have sex in public and so on.
Almost as if she was bragging. And weird shit
about her family, too—some really weird shit, I
never knew what to believe. She made them
sound like the Addams Family of Marin
County, but, you know, Chris was a great
storyteller, you always got the sense that she
was exaggerating like hell. I remember some
story about her dad and various women he
supposedly kept stashed away, on a, I don't
know, a yacht or something, it was really
funny the way she told it. And one night,
when she'd been doing, like, major shots of
tequila, she said something about her mother,
how her mother had never wanted children.
She said—and I've never forgotten this because
it kind of shocked me, it was such a gross
thing to say—she said that she, Chris, was
surprised she hadn't been born with a wire
hanger sticking out of her head, that's how

much her mother had wanted kids. I mean,
that's really such a sick thing to say.

But you never knew which way it was going
to go with Chris, especially when she was
drinking: sometimes she'd be really funny and
sparkling, just excellent company, and other
times you'd feel as if she wasn't there, like
she'd just disappeared inside herself and was
staring out at you from a big black hole.

What do *I* think happened? Well, I think
. . . Hello? Hello? Can you hear me? Shit, I
think we've gone and lost the line. Hello?

With no other body in it, my bed seemed to have
grown vast and perilous, as if, once I drifted to
sleep, there'd be nothing to stop me rolling off the
edge. So, every night, for ballast, I'd take on a fair
quantity of wine, plus, I admit, the occasional dose
of diazepam. Hence, I suppose, the nightly mess of
dreams. Blood and meat; eviscerations of various
kinds.

One morning I woke to find the sheets bedaubed
with blood. It took me a second to understand
why—at first I thought my dreams had soaked
through my sleep—but then I performed some
mental arithmetic on the spot. Twenty-five times
twelve, more or less, how many circuits of the
moon? Three hundred, which meant I'd had, let's

say, that many cycles in my life. I'd have, perhaps, one hundred more. And for what? To watch my dark blood drain out every month, to see it flow into the water like red smoke. An emergency flare: so much tissue wasted, so much time.

Forgive me, I don't mean to sound maudlin, but that's the kind of thought that does occur, occasionally, to women in their thirties. Late thirties. Even women who've chosen, as I have, to remain childless.

I don't mean to stray from the subject, either, so let me resume. Dreams: every night, after a few thin hours of sleep, I'd awaken with a start, sweat-soaked and toxic with fear, my hair clinging in damp strands to my neck, my arms struggling as if straitjacketed against the sheets.

I dreamt that I was peeling the skin off a cat, which turned its head in puzzlement to watch. I dreamt that my nipples oozed a thick white sap— but it was pus, not milk. I dreamt that a killer was nailing me to the floor, hammering nail after nail into me because I took too long to die.

Waking from that one, I knew there'd be no more sleep. The sky outside was still opaque, but I climbed out of bed and turned on the lights, feeling weak and queasy, as if irradiated by the dream. I wrapped my bathrobe around me, then huddled, chin on knees, in front of the TV, trying to decode a soap opera in Spanish. (Why was the lab technician in such distress? And what was inside the red vinyl bag?) Then, as the light paled and the city birds began to squawk, I heard the news deliverer's car, the thud of the paper on the step below.

Another war had broken out in Africa. A Peruvian poet had died. A woman had been killed with a ball-peen hammer two blocks from me.

The print began to jiggle, jitter before my eyes, as if something were wrong with the vertical hold. On reality, not TV.

The woman, a twenty-three-year-old student, had, I believe, been abducted from a laundromat late Tuesday night. Her body, discovered near the river by a rollerblader, was naked and brutally battered, with her own tights knotted around her neck. The hammer blows had been so intense they'd left her brain tissue exposed. The killer's MO, the police chief said, linked this assault to other recent slayings in the area. He appealed for public vigilance, for calm.

There it is: I had dreamt I was being hammered to death at the very moment that a woman *was* in fact being hammered to death, two blocks away.

No, I don't know precisely when that moment was—only a lawyer would ask that—and no, the newspaper didn't say anything about her being nailed to the ground, I'm not claiming to be psychic. Yes of course I've heard of autosuggestion, of cryptamnesia—I took three years of psychology at Berkeley, after all, thinking it might teach me something about the human mind. Yes, I suppose it's at least theoretically possible that I was, as they say, subliminally aware of the first few killings and that that's why I had the hammer dream in the first place.

All I can say is that that's not the way it felt. It felt like a warning of some kind. It felt like information.

WOMAN'S BODY FOUND ON BANK OF CHARLES
Boston Globe, October 22, 1994

The body of a 23-year-old woman was discovered late last night on the bank of the Charles River, by a jogger who noticed a foot protruding from under a canoe. The woman, identified as Sara Lee Gilligan, had been strangled and, according to Police Commissioner Bill Koenig, "beaten about the head with a blunt object, like, say, a hammer or tire iron." Koenig declined to give further details, stating only that the attack had been "pretty brutal" and appeared to be linked to three other recent killings in the area.

Gilligan, an Emerson College junior, had been seen leaving a Kenmore Square laundromat earlier in the evening. The popular young theater major had been expected back at her dorm with a load of clean laundry but, roommates said, she never arrived. Responding to reporters' questions, Koenig said it was "too soon" to know if Gilligan had been sexually assaulted.

"We're still waiting for the lab results," he said, "but, in the meanwhile, please, there's no need to panic. Use your street smarts," he said, addressing Boston's female population, "don't jog alone, and ask to see identification before you open your door to anyone. The Boston Police Department is conducting a thorough investigation."

Around this time, instead of seeking psychiatric help, which in retrospect seems the more sensible recourse, I began to read—voraciously, you might even say compulsively—into the subject of psychopaths, serial murderers and sex criminals in general. Not because, I hasten to add, I believed that anyone I knew fell into such a category—the idea would be nonsensical, deranged, and, besides, I have no desire to defend a libel suit as well—but because . . . Well, because. I don't really know why. A lot of people read those books. For edification, I suppose, and, why not admit it, for the terrible thrill.

I read about the Night Stalker and the Want-Ad Killer, the Mad Bomber and the Son of Sam, the Boston Strangler, the Yorkshire Ripper, the Monster of Florence, and the Beast of the Black Forest. About Heidnik, who kept four women chained in his basement, twisting screwdrivers into their ears when they wouldn't obey. "Society owes me a wife and family," he explained. And about Bundy, who'd had a girlfriend all along, sending her a single red rose every year to mark the day they'd met. He'd also, one Sunday, left the house, abducted a woman from a park, raped and slaughtered her, returned to the park, lured another woman away, raped and killed her too, then headed back to his girlfriend's house for a hamburger and a nap.

When you read something like that, it makes you wonder, that's all. About the stranger in your own life, in your own bed. About the foreign body that your own body has so tenderly admitted, opening around it like the lips of a wound.

SOMETIMES, WHEN HIS body entered mine, I'd open my eyes and look up at him. His eyes would be scrunched shut, his teeth bared, an expression of such savagery that I was afraid: I no longer knew who he was. My face, I realized, probably looked much the same—savage with pleasure, or with some other deep pang. The body never lies, I'd thought, but I no longer knew which language mine was speaking.

It sent me urgent messages from the cerebellum, via the node of Ranvier, the sheath of Swann. It sent me urgent messages from the heart, via the vena cava. It sent me urgent messages from the skin, from the subcutaneous tissue to the stratum lucidum. And I had no idea what they meant. No idea at all.

WE COULD HAVE, should have, met, talked, resolved—like adults, yes—but we'd never learned how. To talk, I mean. We'd always let our bodies do the talking, his tongue moving inside me, his lips shaping themselves on my skin, my mouth filled with the hard choking syllables of sex. Now, without that language, we were mute.

Unless, of course, he was responsible for the obscene calls. Granted, there's no evidence for this, and I'm at a loss to explain how he could have

obtained my new number—unless it was from Angelica, who might not have understood the gravity
of the situation. I'd stopped by the bar one night to
see her, without, of course, going into unnecessary
details about my personal life—or, come to think of
it, any details at all. (I wish now that I had, but,
really, what would I have said? I felt naked,
ashamed, as if waking from a dream, one of those
dreams full of intense irremediable longings that
leave you as lonely and formless and unfit for life as
a gastropod with its shell pecked off.)

Anyway . . . what was my point? Obscene
calls: yes, I'd received such calls before, what
woman hasn't, and I'll no doubt receive them again,
depending, of course, on where I end up. I've even
made a couple myself, to an uncooperative land-
lady, but that's neither here nor there. In the past
several years, total strangers have called to invite
themselves over, to undergo what sounds like an
asthma attack on the other end of the line, to express a keen interest in licking my pussy, and to
explain what they'd like to do to me with a hunting
knife. So I doubt that a few nasty messages would
have pushed me over the edge. My only question is,
how many coincidences do there have to be before
they cease to be meaningless, before they constitute

a system of significance in their own right? And
why would a random caller have said that he knew
what I liked? That he knew what I liked, bitch, we
bitches were all the same, and he'd give it to me all
right, till I bled?

MY LAWYER—RESPLENDENT today in peacock wool
with gold buttons, she must have been on TV—my
lawyer says there's no need to muddy the waters,
that I should just move on to the next incident I
recall involving the complainant. I'm not trying to
muddy the waters, I tell her; I'm just trying to eluci-
date the defendant's state of mind.

SPEAKING OF MUD: when it rains here, which it's doing now, the roof leaks. In three different spots,
each with its own syncopated plink. Just thought I'd
mention that.

NATURALLY, I STOPPED answering my telephone at
home—that's what machines are for: not to communicate with other human beings but to ensure that
you never have to deal with them at all—so, out of

frustration, Scott began besieging Weisner, Bickey, & Taft again, giving a different name to Rosa each time he called. That's why, I suppose, she doesn't recollect the onslaught, the bombardment by phone. But I recall it all right: I recognized his voice every time and hung up immediately, with a small exasperated plosive sound. Unfortunately, as Mr. Naidoo and Dr. Sanchez have already testified, I also hung up once or twice on actual clients, mistaking them for him.

After a week or so of this, he showed up at my office in person, wearing—I'm serious—a baseball cap and a pair of mirrored sunglasses, in, I assume, some bizarre attempt to disguise himself. Perhaps he, too, was losing his mind. Hoping, apparently, to pass as a delivery boy, he clutched a bunch of bedraggled red carnations from the deli downstairs.

Admittedly, I only saw him for a few seconds, and I might have missed the spectacle altogether if I hadn't, that day, been distracted by a commotion outside my office door. Cursing Rosa for her habit of bantering with the FedEx guy, I leapt up and snatched the door open, just in time to catch Scott (or someone who looked very much like him) in a freeze-frame on the far side, one arm out, palm already curved to grasp the knob. From under his other arm, at a precarious angle, poked the afore-mentioned bouquet, which dripped.

Rosa had stopped in the hallway a few feet be-hind him, her arms splayed in vexation, her face the color of a ripe peach—signs, if you knew how to read them, that she was seriously annoyed.

"I told him . . ." she began.

"It's OK," I said, though it wasn't.

"He wouldn't . . ." she began again.

"It's OK," I repeated, then, turning to him as though he were in fact a delivery boy, asked, "Are these for me? Fine," I continued, my voice begin-ning to rise and crack. "Now why don't you just get the fuck out of here before I call the police?"

I snatched the flowers from his hand, closed the door in his face, slumped numbly for a second, and then dumped the whole wet handful into the waste-paper basket. Not sure what to do next, I sat down and laid my cheek, very carefully, on the cool oak surface of the desk, face to face with the tape dis-penser, with its cruel serrated tongue. I had no urge to weep, but I was afraid that if I lifted my head my inner organs—the dark meat of my liver, the sau-sage-string of my intestines, the green sprig of my gallbladder—would eject themselves, all at once, from my mouth.

Of course he's denied that that was him.
Wouldn't you?

THERE'S JUST ONE thing I want to make perfectly
clear: I didn't want to hurt him. His flesh—hard
and cashew-colored and shockingly smooth—had
given me more pleasure than anyone's ever had.
His soft mouth had sucked me into a frenzy. And
the intimacy of his gaze had produced an effect on
me akin to what I imagine is meant by—go ahead,
laugh—by *swooning*, a voluptuous vertigo that
leaves you clinging by the fingernails to the cliff
edge of self. So why, I ask you, should I have
wanted to hurt him?

I didn't want to hurt him. I had no intention of
hurting him. But why, then, wouldn't he leave me
alone? Why did he make those calls? Why did he
sneak into my apartment while I was at work and
rearrange my collection of African carvings, so that
the woman's head ended up in the crocodile's
mouth? Why did he leave a tattered Halloween
mask on the hood of my car? Why? Does it make
any sense to you?

Yes, it's been pointed out to me, and not always
in the most constructive of ways, that there's a

clinical term that might account for the above phenomena. When applied to the defendant, I mean, not the complainant. Well, there are probably several, but you know the one I mean.

Call it what you like. But allow me to ask whether it's possible to live in the city—the post-civilized American city—without contracting that condition to some extent. What do you call it, for instance, when you walk into a department store and find yourself spooked by a presence in your peripheral vision? It's just a mannequin, of course, but that's how they deter shoplifting—by making you feel that you're being watched all the time. What do you call it when, on the subway train, a homeless woman fixes her red-rimmed eyes on you and screams "Don't look at me, bitch! Look at your own cunt! It's drying up!"—and you wonder how she knows? What do you call it when you notice, with dread, a shopping cart upturned in an empty lot, like a skeleton in the desert; an ironing board dumped in an alley, its four white legs extended like limbs?

ONE LAST THING. Around this time, the time of the phone calls and so on, I began to receive a slew of mail from the National Center for Missing Children. Every day, more missing children. Mail from cruise companies, too—implying that I should go away— and from dating services—implying, perhaps, that I should avail myself of one. Coincidences? Maybe.

Surely everything means something; the question is, what?

MY LAWYER, WHO seems to be losing her veneer of professional patience, has instructed me to get a move on, if I would. To the night of the assault. Alleged assault, she says, though, really, I can't imagine why she bothers. Oh, I know she's only doing her job. And, as a fellow professional, I appreciate, of course, the fine job she's doing. It's just that, what can I say, these interruptions, these corrections, these endless requests for clarification are beginning to get on my nerves. Not to mention the constant dripping sound. Someone's dog bleating neurotically in the distance. The way she clicks her pen, a nervous Bic.

What I mean is: I don't think I can do this. Even if I wanted to, I'm not sure I could. My memory still has a piece chewed out of it, a hole, a, what do you call it, a scotoma.

* * *

FIRST LET ME note, by way of preface, that none of
this would ever have happened if the complainant
hadn't lived in such a shoddy loft, with such make-
shift carpentry. On such flimsy constructions do our
fates depend.

All right. That's the end of the preface. We now
move on to the last week of October.

During the last week of October, the complainant
left several messages on my answering machine,
using, for a change, his own voice and leaving, for a
change, his own name. All these messages, which I
ignored, were to the effect that he needed his "toolbox" back. Having, perhaps, read too much Freud
at Berkeley, I at first interpreted them as his—admittedly odd—way of alluding to some profound
sense of emasculation. Only after the fourth or fifth
such call did I realize that they meant exactly what
they said: that the complainant, Mr. R. Scott
DeSalvo, was requesting the return of one large
black metal toolbox that he had left at my apartment several weeks earlier, after assisting in a
home improvement project.

Well, I recognize a gambit when I hear one—

toolbox, indeed—so I didn't respond. Only on the third or fourth call did he mention anything about the bathroom ceiling, and I ignored that too, reasoning that if the problem had indeed been severe, he would have said so from the start. How was I to know that several ceiling panels had in fact come loose? Or that, as he now claims, he was concerned about asbestos particles from the ducts above? Even if he did mention it, which I truly don't recall, you'll understand that I was hardly in a receptive frame of mind. Also, why shouldn't I admit it, I was afraid that if I saw him again, something would happen, something irrational, hormonal, and I'd find myself in his arms again, perhaps even with a sob.

You may be wondering by now what the complainant's problems with ceiling maintenance have to do with the charges at hand. Only this: that he threatened to come over and retrieve his property, whether I liked it or not, and that, on the night of October 31, he did precisely that.

Let this be yet another lesson, by the way, in the virtue of self-sufficiency. If I'd owned my own drill, my own drill bits—my own pilot bit, twist bit, and all the rest—none of this would have happened. My shelves would be up, he would be unharmed, and I would be . . . whatever I was before. Sad, isn't it, when you think how simple things could be. *Have been.*

Enough: if I look back now, look down, second-guess myself, I'll freeze. So let me move directly to the evening in question, October 31, a Tuesday I believe, on which occasion I retired to bed rather early—ten-thirty or so. Perhaps I'd been drinking, I don't recall. It had become, by then, a nightly necessity but what the hell. An hour or so later, I awakened, with a start, to a sound I identified as my doorbell, or, more precisely, the buzzer from the foyer downstairs. Though my heart was pounding, thickly, sickly, I decided to ignore it and not even look out the window to see who was buzzing, having, of course, a pretty good hunch. After three or four more blasts—some, I might add, unnecessarily prolonged—there was, at last, silence: the loud silence of the city night. And that, I thought, was that.

Naturally, I was too agitated to sleep, but I pulled the quilt up under my chin and lay back—nerves tingling, eyes poached open like eggs, pinpoints of light popping in the dark—trying to relax, to breathe. A few minutes later, when I heard something that sounded like footsteps on the stairs, I decided it must be the thump of blood in my own skull. Until, that is, I heard a key turn in the door.

I'd known all along that this would happen, that one day I'd have no way of keeping him out.

I remember leaping out of bed. I remember that I couldn't see very well because I'd taken my contacts out for the night. I remember that he went straight into the kitchen, without turning on any lights, and began opening and shutting the cabinet doors with belligerent slams. That's where, stumbling from the bedroom, I confronted him—wearing, for the record, a faded grey T-shirt and long johns, not, as the police report describes it, "jogging attire." Bare feet. Cold tiles.

If this were a TV docudrama, my repressed memories would come rushing back about now, and I'd be fending off the flashbacks like a swarm of bees. But that hasn't happened yet—which, I won't deny, is a comfort of some kind. Because this isn't a docudrama. It's my life.

There were probably some words, from me, to the effect of what the hell did he think he was doing and would he get out before I called the police. There were probably some words, from him, to the effect that he had come for his toolbox and wasn't going to leave without it. I don't remember the exact words, but I do remember the smell of him, vodka and Camels, with a hint of ozone and exhaust from the air outside. Also, later, something acrid, apocrine.

I opened the broom closet, found the toolbox, told him to take it and go. I handed it to him, I recall, with two hands, from beneath; he took it, I recall, with one hand, from above—don't know why I remember this. He turned as if to leave, toting the box like a workingman on his way to work, an image so incongruous I almost laughed. But then, and I'll never know why, he changed his mind. He stopped, set the box down on the counter, and turned back towards me. As if he wanted something.

The complainant has alleged that, at that moment, I shoved him violently across the room. I may have; I'm not denying it; I just don't recall. I do recall, though, the blinding white-hot bolt that surged through me when I saw him approach, so, yes, I may have. It's not red that you see, by the way, but a kind of supersaturated shimmer, with everything dark and fluctuant about the edges.

I saw him stumble and regain his balance. I heard him curse, saw him turn away, reach for the toolbox. He says—now—that he was planning to pick it up and leave. I thought—then—that he was planning to open it and take something out.

It has of course since been suggested to me, by members of the psychiatric profession, that, under the circumstances—fear, darkness, blurred vision— my senses were, how shall I put it, misinforming me. Perhaps they were. Perhaps all my senses had been misinforming me, lying to me, for quite some time. Perhaps my body had become a pathological liar. But, if so, how would I know? *Have known?* At that moment, I believed it. I would believe it again. And, to tell you the truth, I believe it still.

I saw him open the toolbox, as if to take something out.

What you believe is up to you.

I can't tell you much more, because this is where the hole begins. Not a blackout, no, that would be too easy, but a sucking, swirling sensation, as if my mind were a drain and somebody had pulled the plug. Colors for an instant preternaturally clear and bright. A sense of inevitability, of a physical process that, once under way, can't be arrested—like fainting, like vomiting, like coming, like, I imagine, dying. A sound from somewhere. And then the gap in time, the gap in the self, the irrecoverable absence of mind.

Commonwealth of Massachusetts
Domestic Incident Report

Date of report	Time of report	Date of Occurrence
Nov 1, 1994	0:32 a.m.	Oct 31, 1994

Address of Occurrence
248 Comm. Ave., Apt. 4C, Boston MA 02116

Compl./Victim's Last, First, M.I.
DeSalvo, Reginald S.

Address
445A Harrison Ave., Boston MA 02118

Date of Birth	Age	Race
11/11/68	25	☒ White ☐ Blk ☐ Ind ☐ Asian ☐ Other

Offender/Other Party Last, First, M.I.
Chandler, Christine D.

Address
248 Comm. Ave., Boston MA 02116

Date of Birth	Age	Race:
7/13/56	38	☒ White ☐ Blk ☐ Ind ☐ Asian ☐ Other

Relationship to the Complainant/Victim
☐ Spouse ☐ Parent/Guardian ☐ Friend
☐ Common law spouse ☐ Other relative ☐ Stranger
☐ Child ☒ Other

Offense/Incident Involved:
☒ Fel ☐ Misd ☐ Viol ☐ Other

Any Weapons Used? Threatened? Type:
☐ Yes ☒ No

Any injuries? Describe:

☒ Yes ☐ No   **Lacerations to eyes**

Removed to Hospital? What Hospital?

☒ Yes ☐ No   **Brigham & Womens**

☐ Photos Taken?

☐ Yes ☒ No

☐ Arrest Made?

☒ Yes ☐ No

☐ If Arrest Made, Did Perp. Resist?

☐ Yes ☒ No

Name of witness(es)   Address   Tel

None

Charge(s). List All:

Assault, mayhem, attempted murder

Circumstances of This Case:

☐ Biting ☐ Choking ☐ Destroying Property

☐ Forcible Restraint ☐ Grabbing ☐ Hair Pulling ☐ Homicide ☐ Injury to Child

☐ Kicking ☐ Pulling Phones From Wall ☐ Punching ☐ Pushing

☐ Slamming Into Walls ☐ Sexual Abuse ☐ Slapping ☐ Threats with Weapon(s)

☐ Throwing Items ☐ Using Weapon(s) ☐ Verbal Abuse ☒ Other

Narrative of the Incident

(Reconstruct Occurrence Including Method of Entry & Escape—Include
Unique or Unusual Actions)

**11:56 hrs, radio run: POs Kellogg and Lumiansky
responded to dispute call @ 248 Comm. Ave.
Caucasian female, approx. 5'4", 110 lbs., jogging
attire, admitted officers to building. Kellogg responded
into apt. 4C, found Caucasian male, approx 6', 185
lbs., black jeans, black T-shirt, in crouching position
on kitchen floor. Male had sustained severe injuries to
both eyes, appeared to be in shock due to blood loss.**

Paramedics administered first aid on the scene.
Suspect was determined to be unarmed and taken
into custody.

Victim's Statement of Allegations

No statement

The police report does not specify whether the
toolbox was found open or closed, and, in violation
of procedure, no photographs were made. The police report does specify that the assailant, that's me,
was unarmed. Oh, I know there have been allusions
in the tabloids to "superhuman strength" and "sur-
gical precision" and so on, but—I feel sick but I
can't stop now, this must be said—apparently it's
not that difficult to do what I did. From an anatomi-
cal point of view, I mean. You could do it yourself if
you tried. With your fingernails. The human body, it
turns out, is frighteningly easy to enter. To take
apart.

BASIC HAND STRIKES

• Two finger spear:
Thrown with the index and middle fingers open
and rigid, the last two fingers curled forward,
this technique is used exclusively to the eyes.

• Straight claw/palm heel:
The thumb is in the same position as with the
two finger spear; all four fingers are open and
rigid. Claw forcefully to the eyes and face.

• Thumb gouge:
This technique is often thrown simultaneously
with both hands. In a hitchhike position, plunge
and roll your thumb deeply into your attacker's
eyes.

• Raking claw
The raking claw is used exclusively to the eyes.
This is an open-handed strike that is used in a
flicking manner, with emphasis on accuracy instead of power. With practice, many people can
throw the raking claw with mercurial quick-
ness. It's best not to think of the raking claw as
a finishing blow, but one that will set up your
attacker for his demise.

Here, finally, are the main ideas to keep in
mind. You can only legally fight if:
1. You are in fear for your life.
2. You reasonably believe your assailant has
the capability of harming you.
3. Your assailant has demonstrated intent to
harm you.
4. The danger of grave bodily harm is imminent. You do not, however, have to wait for your
attacker to hit you. Imminent jeopardy means

that you have reasonable cause to feel threatened, and that is justification to strike first.

5. You may legally keep hitting him until he
stops moving and appears to be unable to harm
you.

The rest you know. I've already told you.

I remember the red Sheraton sign on the skyline,
how it throbbed through my window afterwards.
How he lay in silence, his hands pressed to his
bloody face. And how, at that moment, I realized
that I had done something awful, something irrepa-
rable, that my life, as I'd imagined it, was over.
Perhaps, to make myself seem more human, I
should dwell on the remorse that overwhelmed me,
the grueling despair. But I'm trying very hard to tell
the truth. And the truth is that all that came later—
the remorse, horror, heartsickness, despair. (Hence,
of course, the infamous "suicide watch" at McLean,
which I have no desire to discuss here.) But in the
immediate aftermath, as I reached for the phone, I
felt calm, almost, I'm afraid to say, jubilant. Not
because I'd hurt him, no. No. Not that. But because,
I suppose, the damage had finally been done, the
mess had finally been made, and, whatever happened, I'd have nothing more to fear.

I remember dialing 911. You may have heard

the tape by now, my terrible *sang froid*. I remember the fire engine pulling up in the street below, the wheeze and lament of its brakes. I remember the ambulance rocking around the corner on two wheels.

I remember running downstairs to let the paramedics in, and how, as I opened the door, the cold night's clarity bit into my brain. They wore, for some reason, bright blue gloves.

"There's been an accident," I told them, "fourth floor."

"There's been an accident," I repeated to the cop who sauntered from his car, belly first, hands slung into belt. "Bad accident. Fourth floor. Me."

Please note that: *me*. My doing. I've never denied it.

On the way up the stairs, the cop asked if there'd been a domestic dispute, not an unreasonable question, given the locale and my bare feet, bruised arms, and so on. Sort of, I said. What, he wanted to know, was my relationship to the injured party? Good question, I said, not meaning to be flip. Then—from the cold, I suppose—I began to shudder, convulsively, spasmodically, teeth chattering so hard I couldn't speak.

His partner—blonde chignon, brusque manner,

no small talk—escorted me down to the police car, where I continued to shiver. I expected her to hand-cuff me but she didn't. Nobody ever did, as a matter of fact. We waited in the car until the ambulance left, shrieking. Then the first cop climbed back in, and we took off, hot-rodding the cruiser, for no apparent reason, over the median strip. By the time we reached the Berkeley Street station, a reporter from the *Herald* was waiting on the steps.

I'd telephoned for an ambulance, not a police car, of course, but for some reason the city of Boston always sends all three—police, fire, ambulance. Don't know why. Perhaps it's because people can't always tell what kind of help they need.

BACK BAY ATTORNEY HELD IN
BRUTAL ATTACK
Boston Herald, November 1, 1994

Christine Chandler, 38, an attorney at the prestigious Boston firm of Weisner, Bickey, & Taft, was arrested early this morning on charges of assault. The charges stem from an incident late last night in which the Harvard-trained lawyer allegedly assaulted Reginald DeSalvo, 25, during a domestic dispute in Chandler's Back Bay apartment. Chandler, who police say was unarmed, allegedly caused grievous bodily harm to DeSalvo by gouging both his eyes from their sockets. Police would release no further details on the gruesome attack or on the extent of DeSalvo's injuries.

DeSalvo, a reporter for Things magazine, was admitted to Brigham and Women's Hospital, where he remains in serious but stable condition. Chandler, who has allegedly confessed to the attack, remains in police custody, pending psychiatric evaluation. A police spokesman said that investigators have "no idea" what relationship, if any, existed between Chandler and DeSalvo, or what motivated the attack. "Our investigation has only just begun," the spokesman said.

One last thing: When I was taken down to the Berkeley Street police station for fingerprinting— they had to wipe the gore off first with wads of paper towel, oh God—I remembered how, in another life, I'd accompanied a Guatemalan client to the Federal Building to have her own prints done.

And how, as I'd watched her wait her turn, I'd experienced a kind of envy, coveting the calm, gentle touch of the old Chinese man who sat at his small table and handled nothing but hands. (Not at all, I might add, like the brusque blonde from the Boston PD.)

I watched how, without ever raising his eyes, he took each stranger's hand in his, plying each finger with great delicacy between his own—dabbing it, like a paintbrush, on the ink-pad, placing it onto the chart, and rolling it left and right in its designated box. After each finger had been inked, he coaxed the whole hand open and laid it flat across the page, placing his own over it as if in benediction. Then he nodded, once, and inclined his head in courtly fashion towards a huge can of gel, for cleaning up.

Watching him repeat this impersonal caress, I suddenly longed to be next in line, to feel him press my prints from me, and then, stained palms splayed, to plunge my hands into the gel. I wanted to yield my fingers, one by one, to this mute stranger who would never look at my face, but wouldn't need to, since he could read my skin's secret whorls like a glyph.

* * *

I'VE JUST LOOKED out of the window to see the sun coming up. Sometimes I forget what an astonishing, tender, luminous place the world can be.

THERE ISN'T MUCH more to tell. And what there is has already been told in the papers—along with, of course, heady doses of fantasy and fabrication. As you may know, the trial begins in a month or three, depending on how long it takes to select a jury, a process that, I gather, has become a minor racket in its own right. Even now, I suppose, "focus groups" are gathering before two-way mirrors to determine who, in their right mind, might be sympathetic to my cause.

The problem, as far as I can see, is that I have no cause. Whether my lawyer argues insanity or self-defense, whether the jury declares me a psychic casualty or a putrid human being, I know what I've done. I know what I've done, and I know there can be no excuse, no mercy, no possible absolution. I know what I've done; I just don't know why.

Oh, I have some inkling, of course; over the past

several months, I've not lacked for psychiatric attention, nor am I, I hope, ineducable. And being alone here has given me, for the first time in my life, ample leisure for introspection. You could probably make the diagnosis yourself, after the way I've skinned the onion of my psyche for you. Yes, you or I could probably put a name to my affliction—or his, for that matter—but how would it help? I still wouldn't know, in my heart, what happened.

I still don't know what he wanted from me, nor, to tell the truth, I from him. We'd delegated our bodies to speak for us, to come to some kind of understanding. But it's dangerous to let your body speak for you, I've discovered, because half the time it doesn't know what it's saying.

"What the hell is the matter with you?" he'd once asked, or, rather, yelled, when we were arguing about something, I forget what. "What the hell do you want?"

"A good question," I remember retorting, rage beginning to fizz beneath my ribs. "A good question," I repeated, "I've been wondering much the same thing myself." Then, realizing what I'd said, I added, lamely, "About you, I mean."

Perhaps everything would have been simpler if I'd been able to answer that question. Using common four-letter words, like *want* and *need*. Perhaps—but it's too late now.

I don't know what will become of me, nor, I must confess, do I really care. Whatever my sentence, I doubt it could be bleaker than the time I've already served in solitary, some thirty-nine years. So my future prospects don't keep me awake at night; I'll accept, without demur, whatever punishment comes my way.

What does torment me, what makes me writhe and moan through the long insomniac nights, is the question of what will become of him. I can hardly bear to think of what I've done; in some ways, it might have been kinder to have killed him. I've often considered imitating Oedipus—his act of atonement, I mean, not his domestic relations. But afterwards the earth was kind enough to open up and take the blind king in. There's no guarantee that that would happen to me. So, with medication, I make it through the days, and, with different medication, occasionally through the night.

There've been no revelations, no epiphanies, I'm afraid, just a chronic yearning for everything to have been different, most of all my self. But the other night, in a rare, barbiturate-induced dream, he did appear to me. His face was mercifully in shadow, his arms outstretched, as if, once again, he wanted something. And I realized, please don't laugh, that he needs someone to take care of him now. To tend to him, possibly for the rest of his life.

And why, I wondered as I woke up, shouldn't that someone be me?

ACKNOWLEDGMENTS

I would like to acknowledge my indebtedness to the following sources: *Defend Yourself! Every Woman's Guide to Safeguarding Her Life*, by Matt Thomas, Denise Loveday, and Larry Strauss (Avon, 1995), and *No! No! No! A Woman's Guide to Personal Defense and Street Safety*, by Kathy Long with Davis Miller (Perigee, 1993).

For their generosity with their time and professional expertise, I would like to thank Laurie B. Riccio, Esq., Felice J. Batlan, Esq., P.O. Mary Ellen Donohue, and Dr. Patricia Normand.

For shelter and sustenance of various kinds, I would like to thank Ruth Butler, Thomas Bass and Bonnie Krueger, Emilia Dubicki, Maurice Isserman and Marcia Williams, Win Pescosolido and Linda Pescosolido, Demos and Aspa Stavropoulos, Edward Wheatley, and Mary Mackay.

And, above all, I'd like to thank my editor, Betsy Lerner.